HellBurger

David P. Holmes

North Star Press of St. Cloud, Inc.
Saint Cloud, Minnesota

Cover image: Jeff Holmes

ISBN: 0-87839-585-7
ISBN-13: 978-0-87839-585-9

First Edition, June 2011

Printed in the United States of America

Published by
North Star Press of St. Cloud, Inc.
P.O. Box 451
St. Cloud, Minnesota 56302

www.northstarpress.com

HellBurger

Also by David P. Holmes

Fiction:
Secrets
Emily's Run
Loose Gravel

Non fiction:
Salt of the Earth

Contact with the author is welcome through his website
www.davidpaulholmes.com

HellBurger

Chapter One

My name is Norbert Klein and I prefer to be called Norby. I'm a private eye, and my business is rounding up bad guys, snooping on cheaters, serving subpoenas to people who don't want them, all while trying to avoid being arrested myself. If a person needs to find me, it helps being a young attractive babe. I avoid the rest of the population as much as possible. I used to have a thriving business in a swank suburb of Minneapolis, but I got too involved with a client. It was a downhill trip after that, and I landed here.

Duluth, Minnesota, Superior Street.

What I hate most about waking up is knowing I'm not dead and I had another day to face. Shit, shower, shave, and look for something to keep me busy. I know it's daytime because the sun is slamming through the rip in the window shade. The last time I tried to fix the shade it fell on me, so now I treat it with a disdainful respect and leave it alone. The duct tape I used to mend the rip is hanging loose, curled over itself, absolutely useless. Daytime and sunshine were meant for tourists and happy people, of which, I am neither.

Getting my legs to fall over the side of the bed was a good step to start the getting-up routine. Forcing my fifty-year-old body into an upright position took more effort than I was willing to invest, and gravity won, pulling me back down to wait for Brooklyn Decker to come and help me up. I had her picture around here someplace.

This was no good and was only starting to hurt more. "Uhn. Oh shit." *Yeah, good boy, you're doing it. A little more and…* "Phew, why do I do this?" Every day, the same thing. Looking over to the other side of my bed I needed to confirm whether or not I was alone. Evidently, whoever I tried to pick-up last night had been too smart or not desperate enough.

Shuffling to the bathroom I could feel the grit on the floor embedding into my feet. "I gotta tell the butler to at least sweep." At the sight of the toilet right where it was supposed to be, I enjoyed the first satisfying function of the day. Things were looking better when I discover there was hot water.

In as good a condition as possible, I washed out the toothpaste residue with a swill of Old Mr. Boston. "*AHHHGGH.*" I swallowed and grimaced until the pain subsided. If I took time to make coffee, it'd mean I was cooking, and I didn't do that. Not that I couldn't if I really wanted to, though. Last time I tried making coffee, I had discovered a mouse in the pot. The little grubber was running in circles trying to get out. And it had shit all over the bottom of the pot. I left him alone. A few days later he was gone, somehow, but the little black things remained. And, as far as I know, still do.

My apartment, on the second floor of an old brick building in fashion before I was born, had an abandoned appliance store on the ground floor. It was a haven for derelicts too proud or drunk to go to a shelter. My friend Hankey lived there. He was a societal drop-out who found satisfaction and comfort living in squalor with more drop-outs just like himself. I didn't know if I was surprised or disappointed when I learned he had a master's degree from some Ivy-league college out East. Listening to one of his rambling dissertations on the evils of the world, he let slip that he used to be a lawyer in a big New York office. He said he left his wife, but I had a hunch he killed her and was hiding. He got hung with the moniker "Hanky" when I heard his name was Homer. Clever twist, huh? I kept his friendship with a constant supply of muscatel, Silver Satin, and Mad Dog. With his connection to the sewers of Duluth, I had a pipeline to the dealings of whatever scum was moving at the time. In my line of work, that was an important element.

One of the features of my home was the fire escape on the alley side. I used it once when a guy was giving chase, trying to kill me. Totally stupid on the use of fire escapes, I fell, breaking my foot. The guy with the gun was probably still laughing at me. His thinking was accurate—I wouldn't be hitting on his wife anymore. Now I boldly exited where any respectable or smarter man left—through the front door. Stumbling down the hallway, I thought I should move the bed out there. It was as dark as a pig's butt, and smelled no better, but it was perfect for sleeping with no intrusion from the morning sun.

Over the dead odors permeated into the walls and thread-bare carpet, I could smell bacon burning in the Feldstein apartment. If I hurried I could bypass the puking stage of not liking it before Mrs. Feldstein discovered me and insisted on fattening me up. She was an irritating, extremely heavyset old lady, but she'd earned a level of respect with me and I'd learned to love her.

When she talked about the numbers tattooed on her forearm and what she had needed to do stay alive in Auschwitz sixty years ago, I figured I could at least be nice to her. Why she was cooking bacon was none of my business. Maybe she found a way to make it kosher. Her husband had died a few years ago and left her with nothing but his contribution to Social Security. She was living on a rental subsidy, and seemed to be accepting of her fate.

Once out on Superior Street, I was blinded by the brightness again. "Man, that hurts." Most people sentenced to a lifetime in Minnesota think sunglasses were meant for snow glare. That was true to a degree, but on a day like this they could ward off a serious headache by blocking that bright obnoxious crap shinning down. Fortunately, sunny days in Duluth were a rarity.

I needed to get something coursing through my arteries besides blood and Old Mr. Boston, so the coffee idea sounded better now. Orienting myself, I shuffled to get my ass over to Canal Park and into the kitchen at HellBurger. For some ungodly reason they didn't open the doors until eleven a.m., so I had to sit in the kitchen. The owner, Mitch Omer, gave me the okay to show up early because I was too much of a pain in his ass to deny access. He was maybe trying to upgrade his image by keeping me hidden.

Mitch wasn't around to yell at me, so I stole a cup of coffee and found my usual chair in the corner. If I didn't get in the way or contaminate anything I'd be treated cordially.

Watching the kitchen staff put together stuff to make normal and healthy people happy, I tried to make casual conversation with anybody who wouldn't throw me out. "Hey, Snotty, how's the missus?" He'd earned the nickname when he'd written down his given handle for me, but his illegible script didn't look anything like "Scotty."

Tossing a piece of garlic bread to me that he'd dropped on the floor, he answered, "My missus? Norby, your memory's as long as your dick. She left me a year ago."

Brushing off the dirt, I downed the slice of bread. Good.

Pondering, "Oh, yeah." I knew but tried to push it aside. Snotty hired me to find out if she was boinking another guy and who. Unknown to the poor man, it was me. Concocting a lie, his wife told him she was a lesbian and left him with nothing but a maxed-out Wal-Mart card. Along with the balance due.

I checked the wall by the door for messages. Luckily, there were none. One more stop before I hit the office. I waved good-bye to no one, because nobody gave a crap if I was there or not.

My next stop held nothing as healthy as the garlic bread, but was more important than food, more important than sex with my picture of Brooklyn Decker, and more important than air—clean or dirty. Strippers. The same as at HellBurgers, my entrance to the Conestoga Club was at the rear. Dark as a dungeon just inside the door, I knew my way and let the comfort of the hallway wall keep me from stumbling. Loud and angry voices up ahead didn't deter me a bit. Stepping into the lounge I knew I had interrupted something, but it would take more than that to stop me. A tall naked blonde girl brushed past me and told me to have sex with myself. Not a bad idea.

Approaching a hairy man who looked like King Kong, I said, "G'morning, Louie. Honing your diplomatic skills?" I nodded in the direction of Blondie's exit.

"Hey, Norby. I thought you was in jail." Louie's voice was a direct contradiction to his appearance but fit perfectly with his sexual orientation. High pitched and almost musical. I heard him sing once, and it had brought me to melancholy tears. His act of being the product of Godzilla's loins was a cover to his fagginess. However, once you were in his good graces, you had a friend who would die for you. Or at least fake death. We got close when I took a bullet meant for him. He called me a hero, but actually, I stumbled trying to run away from the hooker trying to kill him for firing her. Dancing nude for entertainment was one thing; selling sex on the dance floor was a reason for the city to close a place down.

"Naw, that was last week. What's shakin' 'cept your fat belly?"

"Fuckin' hookers, man. They all want to start a whorehouse in here."

"Gee, why would a hooker want to start a whorehouse? That why Blondie huffed off?"

He nodded and shrugged, saving his words for something more important. Reaching over the bar, he came back with a napkin still soggy from whatever. I sniffed it, and not smelling like urine, decided it was okay to touch. The ink had blotted but the message was still legible. "What's this?"

Shrugging his massive frame, he muttered, "What? I'm your secretary now? I took the goddamn message. Now you got it." Walking away he called back in an irritating whine, "That's okay, you don't have to pay for it. Don't worry. I'll take care of the shit stuff for you. I don't care. Go ahead and take advantage of me. That's okay."

"What? Louie, you on the rag again? Take a pill, man."

His response told me what my next move would be. "Go on, get the fuck out of here."

If my car hadn't been rusted and full of dents, it'd be a classic. To me, the '85 Plymouth Reliant was beautiful. The radio worked if I was in a strong signal area, it didn't drip too much oil, and the blanket covering the ripped and blood-stained back seat just added class. I impressed people by telling them the blood was the result of a dangerous, intriguing case I'd solved. Truth? I'd picked up a woman with the hots for a man, any man. She was panting and wrestling her way to an orgasm, when suddenly, she exploded with her period, all over me and my classic Plymouth. The rip came from her high heel digging into my custom upholstery.

My office belied my living condition. Located near the posh Miller Hill area, I rented a small space next to a respectable vitamin store. The place was big enough for two rooms, one for me and one for my right hand, Jeanine. No, that wasn't what I meant. She's a real woman—her name is Jeanine. Jesus, cut me some slack.

Jeanine's area was warm, clean, brightly lit, and smelled of incense or some other smelly-nelly stuff. Her desk looked like a display in an up-scale furniture showroom, shining like a new apple. Her pencils, paper clips, stapler, and the other officey-type crap were arranged in military fashion in the properly assigned area. Even her computer was artsy-fartsy—a laptop worth more than my classic Plymouth. But, according to Jeanine, her toothbrush was worth more than my car. I felt people came into the office just to absorb the genuine leather guest chairs and read *Architectural Digest, National Geographic,* and the *Wall Street Journal.* I kept the good mags in my desk.

Due to the condition of my office, Jeanine insisted on keeping the door closed as a barrier between two separate states of attitude. I won't even bother with a full description of my office. I've already mentioned my living quarters, so why duplicate.

However, in case you're curious, my desk is gray metal, which I take pride in noting it matches two of my filing cabinets. My Acer computer—a desk ornament—is as classic as the Plymouth. The reason why the monitor's so big—that's the way they made them back then. My two, no three, guest chairs don't match in any way. And that third one just kind of showed up. I'd never seen that one before. The only functional drawer in the desk was the large bottom right one. Just tall enough for a bottle of Canadian hooch. Nothing but the best. I prefered to label my decorating taste as eclectic.

I carefully laid the damp but drying napkin on the linoleum surface of my classic desk, carefully tracing the number so I could actually be confident of it being a phone number. Knowing Louie, it could be a connection to a phone sex operation. My hopes went up that it might just be that.

Jeanine lived in a spirit world. She floated in an element unknown to mere mortals. We seldom talked because she'd always known what to say and what the answer should be. She strode into my office with a sneer, afraid of touching anything, sure of some unidentified disease.

Her first words of the day, "Morning, Norbs. Yes, the number's legitimate. I'm the one who called your strip club office annex in hopes that you'd actually use the number to get a job so you could make payroll."

Looking up, searching for her face but lingering on her breasts, I said, "Well, good morning, Jeanine. How are you today?"

She set a fresh cup of coffee in front of me. "If I had written it on my boobs you wouldn't have to ask, you dope."

I tolerated her caustic attitude and sharp piercing tongue because I was afraid of her. She held a black belt in about seven oriental martial arts skills, was rated an expert target shooter, pitched in a women's softball league, and lifted weights. From the floor to the top of her head she was a collection of curves that went in and out just in the right places. And she smelled like apricots. Her hair was the color poets talked about when they waxed eloquent about a warm day in Kansas, kind of honey-straw blonde. Long enough to sway when she walked, today it was kept confined in a pony tail. She wore it loose once when she went to Starbucks for a femmie-wemmie latte or something, and dragged three studs back with her. She made a date with one of them, but he was never seen again. Her eyes, well, I didn't look at them. I'd never be the same again.

I put a move on her once and had to go in for an ex-ray and a chiropractic realignment. Responding to her greeting, I countered with, "Yes, sir. Thank you, sir."

Bravely sitting in one of my guest chairs, she crossed one of those marvelous legs over her other knee, and told me, "The message is from Adelle Pierpont, connected to none other than the London Road Pierponts. She wants you to do some sleuthing for her."

"Sleuthing?"

"Yes, that's known as doing detective work. Like in getting paid to be a detective. I grilled her to be sure she didn't have the wrong number, you being you and all, and she was definite about wanting none other than Norbert Kline."

"Did you ask her to call me Norby?"

"No, I told her to call you shit head. Now, make the call and write me a pay check."

• •

Adelle Pierpont lived in one of those ornate castles that sat on the shoreline of Lake Superior, just out of the bustling Duluth business hub-bub. The traffic on London Road was non-stop, busy and noisy, but the royalty that owned the lakeshore property seemed to have enough clout to order the noise and confusion to stop at their property lines. The tourists pulling fifth-wheels and tent trailers were no different from the rest of the travelers. They all had their heads stuck out the window hoping for a glimpse of a rich guy, preferably someone recognizably famous. Most of the obnoxious ogling public was absorbed by the Glensheen mansion and its ghostly tale of murder and mayhem.

Jeanine broke the ice for me and called to announce the arrival of Norbert Kline, detective and process server. On my embossed business card, I had added the title "pimp" to the copy that went to the printer, but it was intercepted by my secretary, Kung Foo Jeanine. I was stuck with legitimate jobs.

Risking my life, and the preservation of my Reliant, by crossing the heavy traffic on London Road, I pulled up to the black iron gates in front of the Pierpont extravaganza. I sat looking at a large ornate "*P*" attached to the metal bars, wondering what had to happen to get them open. My mindset on open-sesame was interrupted by a loud, irritating voice squawking from outside the car. My response was, "Shut up, I can't think."

When I realized the voice was saying, "Mr. Kline, please push the red button," it took a long moment to understand just what was meant by, *push the red button.* As dumb as a stump, I sat looking at the red button a good minute before my mind connected the dots. Duh!

Naturally, the red fucking button was about a foot out my reach. Pushing my two-hundred-twenty pounds through the one-fifty capacity window of the Plymouth, I had to do a Laurel and Hardy act to reach it. Stretch, yeah, oh shit, yeah and *got it.* Struggling to avoid proving gravity was the smarter of the two of us, I managed to get my bulk back in through the window. "Phew."

More loud commands from the stupid black box. I knew I couldn't get to the button again and maintain any form of dignity, but, fortunately, I didn't have to. "Mr. Klein, please proceed to the portico."

Still a dumb stump, I gazed in awe as the large mass of iron slowly yawned open to accept my classic Plymouth. Portico?

While the Reliant dieseled itself to a stop, I stood in front of a towering pair of doors that probably cost more than I had ever earned in my life. One door silently swung inward to reveal a woman I hoped was not the maid. My perception of a household servant was a squat woman dressed like a pilgrim in a black ruffled dress with white trim. The lady who stood by the door was hardly that. If I were to invent a word to describe elegance, grace, beauty, wealth, snob, and extreme hot babe, she would be it.

While Jeanine is an out-and-out stone-cold sex-laden fox, this vision standing before me was soft lights, sophistication, tiny lacy underwear, and breath-taking. About five-foot nine, soft blonde hair with each strand precisely pulled tightly back and captured by a wide gold barrette. I'm sure I could hock the thing and pay my electric bill. Her construction was formed into a killer ass, abs, and boobs, with legs that were nothing less than a cello sonnet. A tight cashmere sleeveless dress was painted on her, giving the color beige a whole new status.

I was being hypnotized by the deep-brown eyes when I started acting like a business man again and broke the spell. My inclination was to step back and ward her off by thrusting my fingers in the sign of the cross at her, but being too suave and genteel, I simply willed my tongue to soften enough for me to speak.

"Mrs. Pierpont?" My voice was hoarse and filled with pubescence.

The vision in beige extended a long soft arm with a hand, complete with fingers, molded to the end of it. A simple chain of gold hung loosely, adorning the wrist, and I wanted to eat it. The wrist. At this level of sophistication, evidently shaking hands was uncouth, and I didn't dare get close enough to kiss it. In perfect form, she let her fingers drape in my hand, and then pulled away. That act alone was worth the trip over here.

Her lips parted and I could only imagine all the wonderful things she could do with them. "No, I'm her daughter, Kathleen. Adelle is in the study. Follow me, please." Her voice was soft, and I could imagine it smelled like baby powder.

I had no idea if the large front door had been shut or not, but I was led like a puppy behind her, mesmerized by the two soft round mounds of butt flesh as they worked in unison. I didn't care where we were going as long as this trip never ended. My God, she was beautiful. For an instant, the vision of Cheryl shot through me, making me ashamed of myself. More about that later.

The interior of the Pierpont manor was hushed and serene, adorned by warm dark woodwork and deep plush carpeting. She stopped at what she must have referred to as "the study." Not being so gauche as to actually make a fist, her fingers tapped lightly on the door before opening it. Floating into the room, she beckoned me to follow. I didn't know if I was broadcasting my feelings to her, but I'd follow her through snake shit and eat ground glass if she asked.

Baby Powder spoke. "Adelle . . . Mr. Klein." I guess when one swims in money and sophistication one never calls parents by the terms *ma* or *pa*. My old man was simply, "my old man." Kathleen's mother was labeled "Adelle."

Adelle Pierpont was sitting in a straight-backed upholstered chair, her hands neatly folded in her lap. To me, gray hair was just a head growth that had died. On Adelle Pierpont it looked like it was waiting for a royal crown to be set on it. Deep silver, almost gun blue, but not obvious. Of course, to my keenly honed powers of observation, I caught on right away. A dark-blue suit-type thing, trimmed in white, covered a body that was obviously at one time, well-toned, neat, prim, and proper. As though it was meant to be hidden, I caught a glimpse of an ornate cane resting against the opposite side of her chair. The silver head curled gracefully and the gnarled cane shaft would be out of place anywhere but here.

When she decided I was worth addressing, her voice was surprisingly deep and strong. "Mr. Klein, please sit down." It was not an offer, but a command with a bit of politeness attached to it.

I lowered myself onto a short couch called a settee. I knew that because I saw one in the Goodwill once. Her highness glanced at the babe, who had also taken a seat, and said, "Kathleen?" I couldn't tell if it was a question or a statement.

In an amazingly quick motion Kathleen was up, telling us, "I'll leave you two alone now." With the grace and mysterious motion of smoke, she was up and out the door. As she closed it I caught a glimpse of her looking at me. I was sure I'd turned her on and she wanted me now.

Brought to attention, Mrs. Pierpont asked, "Would you care for anything? Coffee? Tea?"

I wanted to ask if she would mind if I went after Kathleen, but only responded, "No, no thank you."

"Just as well. Let's get down to business." She reached to a small table next to the chair, picked up an envelope, and handed it to me. "If that's not enough, let me know."

Without opening it, I knew it was more than enough. Just paying for the gas to get here would have been more than I had made all month. Attempting to be businessy and polite, I muttered, "I'm sure it will be . . ."

She cut off what surely would have been prattling. "Yes, I'm sure. Now, you're here because nobody knows you. You're kind of a non-entity and don't have enough pride to turn down a job. Especially this one."

On the one hand, my inclination was to reach over and smash her face for the disparaging comment, but the envelope was vibrating in my hand. She was right.

Assured it was understood that she was in charge, and I was slime. She went on. "I want complete secrecy with this matter. I will not tolerate any indiscretions. Do you understand?"

The little self-respect I had started to boil. Leaning forward, thinking I should hand back the envelope but knowing better, I said, "Why don't you just tell me what you want."

She paused, appearing to second guess telling me anything. She glanced at the door, then said, "I want you to spy on my husband. I think he's having an affair."

Oh, is that all? "What makes you think so?"

Waving her fingers in the air, she brushed off my question, "I just do. However, I don't care who he's fucking. I only want to make certain he doesn't get caught and have the whole thing show up in the paper." Hesitating again, she went on, "Then, there's the matter of something that . . . let's just say, something he has that needs to be in my hands."

Thinking the amount in the envelope might not be enough after all, I said, "Okay. I'll find out who he's boinking, make sure it stays out of the society page, and find out where whatever it is turns up. What is it?"

For the first time she looked straight into my eyes, and I think I'd rather get shot. Steely gray and fierce—I felt as if I was being subjected to Kryptonite. "You don't need to know that."

I tucked the envelope into my coat pocket, thinking at least I'd get something for sitting through her game. "Mrs. Pierpont, I need to know what I'm looking for if I'm supposed to find it."

"When you spy on Elwood, you will no doubt uncover what he's hiding."

Elwood? Pierpont was snobby enough for a name, but why would anybody name a kid Elwood? "Any hints? The longer this takes, the more it's going to cost."

"Mr. Klein, does it look like I care about how much you milk out of me? Now, sit back, and I'll give you some starters to locate him."

CHAPTER TWO

I LISTENED TO THE OLD LADY FOR OVER AN HOUR tell me what an ungrateful blood-sucking asshole her husband was. What I learned was that the Pierpont money was hers and he held his social status because of her generosity. Old money, old people, old values. They had more money than they need and spent it making more. There was never enough. Elwood's philandering had been going on for years, and he was always bailed out by the queen. This time there was something attached to it that I was supposed to find, but I had no idea what it was.

Whatever Elwood was involved in I hoped it was a local concern. According to Adelle, he had been a U.S. diplomat stationed in the Far East—Arabia, or some other Muslim place. He was retired, but her inference of his dabbling as a freelance could mean this thing could go to a level I didn't want to see.

In a typical Adelle Pierpont manner, she indicated she had told me enough by waving her bony fingers, "Get out of here now. We're done. And don't forget that I want results."

In the hallway, I looked for Kathleen, but she was probably getting undressed waiting for me. I knew which direction the front door was, so for once in my life I used discretion and left.

Happy that the Plymouth started, I went back to the office. Parked in my usual illegal spot, my curiosity finally got the better of me. I pulled out the envelope. *And the winner is . . .* holy shit! I sat paralyzed, looking at a string of zeros, counting five of them, and a great big *one* in front of the two zeros before the comma. One-hundred-thousand fucking dollars. Turning the check over didn't change a thing. One-hundred-thousand dollars and no cents.

Stumbling into the office, I didn't know where to put the check to be sure it was safe. I could tuck it into my shorts, nobody ever went in there.

Dancing into my section of the office, I slid into my caster chair as graceful as Gene Kelly. Giddy and tingling with euphoria, I should have known that I didn't deserve any of it, that it didn't belong to me. My purpose in life was to let others fill me with hope just to have a reason to smash it. This time was no different.

Euphorically floating over my desk, the first thing I saw was a manila envelope with special delivery stickers all over it. Checking the post mark, I saw it came from San Diego. Usually, Jeanine filtered the mail, taking out the junk and pornography. The reason she hadn't open this one scared the crap out of me.

Jeanine, along with her other powers, was psychic. She knew things that ugly humans like myself knew nothing about. I could imagine that by touching this envelope, and knowing where it came from, she would leave it to me. It was my business, and she would interfere if I wanted her to. I wanted her to.

Using my dirty pocket knife, I slit the envelope open, wishing it was junk mail, or better yet, pornography. I looked at the return address before I got enough nerve to look inside. *Marcella Hudson, San Diego, CA.* Pushing it away from me across the desk top, I stared at it before I took out the Grande Canadian and a dirty, stained water glass. "It's going to take more than this." Three fingers of amber ecstasy slid down my throat, giving me courage to look inside.

I was right. It was bad news. No, I take that back. Bad just doesn't describe what it really was. There had to be a place way past "bad" in a spot where hell met "bad." I read, *"Dear Mr. Klein, I'm sorry to write this, but knowing your relationship with my mother, you deserved a note. My mother passed away a few days ago. The tumor that developed from the beatings she took were too much. Mr. Wallace, Roger, and myself were with her to the end. My father never answered our call to him, which is typical. At the end she asked me to tell you that she is sorry things didn't happen the way you wanted. She did care for you very much and asked me to send her love and say goodbye for her.*

Thank you, Jennifer Hudson.

The words to an early Linda Ronstadt song tore through my head, *To remind me once again that I was wrong…*

• •

Jeanine found me the next morning, still planted in my swivel office chair, head on the desk, and my face looked like someone had pissed on it. I was not a sentimental guy and avoid things like Christmas and Easter for fear of looking like a pussy. When Jeanine stepped into my half of the office, I opened up and cried like a baby. She put the Grande Canadian away and tossed the glass into the waste basket. I wondered if I had a straw someplace.

She opened with, "I knew it was from her. I had no business looking at it. Do you want to go out there?"

Wiping my face with a shirt sleeve, I sniffled, "Why? She's gone." A moment later, I was a little more reasonable. "Maybe later. I couldn't handle it now."

She nodded and I handed her the check from Adelle Pierpont. Her eye brows knotted in the middle, and she said the only logical thing, "What? Did you have sex with her? You're not worth this much." She spun around and raced to the bank with a deposit slip and my forged signature.

Pushing back in my chair, nearly scooting across the room, my blurred eyes saw the pictures on my desk, again. Worried I had gotten them wet, I scooted back. Picking both eight-by-tens, I went through the pain once more. The real stabber was with Cheryl. Marci Hudson and Linda Ronstadt were just reminders that, indeed, I was wrong.

• •

All right, my story.

I had been on the Minneapolis police force for twelve years before I quit and got a degree in psychology. Yeah, me, a college graduate. One day while still on the force, my wife, Cheryl, asked me to stay home because she didn't feel good. Well, with all the bad guys on the streets, Norbert Klein was needed to save humanity. "I'll be back later."

When I got home that evening, she was sitting alone in the dark. I'll never forget the conversation that followed.

"Norby, I'm pregnant."

"What? Oh, man, that's great."

"It's not yours."

"What?"

"I'm in love with someone else. It's his baby. I want a divorce."

For the next six or eight months I was the biggest asshole I knew how to be. I hit her, I beat up her lover, and I was constantly drunk and abusive. One day when I heard her crying in the bathroom, I knew I was wrong. I told her how sorry I was and that I wouldn't get in the way. I was in love with her, and I had no right to treat her so badly. It was my fault she looked for love someplace else.

I had made life so miserable for so long that the divorce was tied up with my ramblings and anger. Before Cheryl and what's-his-name could be free to get married, the baby came, and they both died in childbirth. I didn't know how I was going to get over that. To this day, I hadn't. I saw what's-his-name now and then, but the only common ground between us I wouldn't tread on. The final twist of the knife was when the hospital lab confirmed that the baby was indeed mine.

I wanted to die, but that was too easy. I needed to go through hell for what I did. Nothing I could ever do to myself would hurt as much as living with the pain.

Marci Hudson's was a case I took because of the similarity in appearance between her and my wife, Cheryl. I fell in love with Marci, but I was afraid it was a cover for Cheryl. Marci knew that and was smart enough to tell me to go away. I think she did love me, but there were too many things in the way. Like her husband. And her lover.

While I was stewing in my juices and trying to develop a logical plan to get close to Elwood Pierpont to figure him out, someone else got to him before I did.

Chapter Three

His breathing was heavy. He was laboring too hard. For five-hundred dollars, he expected to be sent to heaven, but as usual, this guy was more difficult. He did not like to be led or cajoled, making an issue of being the one who was in control.

Laura made the mistake of letting him drink too much, disabling his senses. If he failed to show his triumph soon, he would make it her fault, and the pimp would be obliged to hurt her again, possibly in front of him to justify not giving his money back.

Reaching down to hold him tightly, she used the other hand to caress his head and cheek. Softly whispering into his ear, "Oh, Elwood, you're so wonderful. I want you more, oh, baby. That's good honey. Keep going."

That had a stimulating effect on him, and she felt his body stiffen. Clenching her legs tighter, she rode with him until the climax. His spasms increased until he fell on her as dead weight, panting, "Oh, shit, that was awesome."

Lifting his head to look at her, he smiled and kissed her lightly. Still panting, he told her, "Laura, you're simply wonderful. You always make it so special."

Smiling, returning the kiss, she said, "I could do this forever with you, Elwood. I think I might be in love with you." Covering her theatrics by massaging his temples, she added, "Got room for another one, honey? I don't want to stop yet."

Holding his head with both hands while her hips slowly gyrated, she could feel the erection come back. Her purpose was to gratify him again, and if she could make it feel good enough, he'd tip her, promising not to tell. For five-hundred dollars, just to have a climax, she could hone her customer service skills to make him want to use her again. His renewed tension and fervor let her know he was getting back on the swing, so she started the act all over.

The grand finale got a recall when she breathlessly pleaded, "Don't stop, Elwood, keep going. I feel it getting to me, honey. I'm coming, oh, God, you're so special."

Her customer was a particular regular, always asking for her. Laura made a special effort to make him feel as if she was his personal girlfriend. Many times they would go out to dinner, or a movie, sometimes just sitting and talking like husband and wife. Tonight, they had dinner at the hotel restaurant before casually moving up to the room.

When her customer was in the arms of the angel, he was the most singular man on earth. He was treated with tenderness and seduction designed especially for him. He was the prince of happiness and was made to feel that making love to Laura was like driving a Maserati Gran Cabrio on the Autobahn, wide open.

The second round was going well, and she pondered faking her orgasm and offering a blow job as a reward. It would be a nice finish to a perfect evening. Until she gazed past her customer's heavy, hairy body and saw movement in the other room. The quiet, sudden presence upset her. She was worried she'd lose her tip. Any money that was passed belonged to the pimp, except when she did a few extra steps to convince the customer to keep her reward a secret.

The shadow passing across the open bedroom door was disconcerting, yet it was obvious it had a purpose being there. But it was too soon. The customer was usually allowed some time to cuddle and fondle before his time was up. This had never happened before and she didn't like it.

The unknown presence slithered into the darkness, illuminated by a dull glow from the other room. Putting additional effort into soothing and stroking her customer, she adjusted her manipulation so Elwood wouldn't falter, or worse, stop. Her mind was racing at light speed, bothered about what she could have done wrong to make whoever it was show up in the middle of a performance. Multiple orgasms were common when she was able to maneuver the customer to such heights of pleasure. This time it was different.

Her flesh had cooled to goose bumps. Maintaining her rhythm, Laura looked up into the eyes of the devil smirking back at her. Panic exploded in her mind. The mattress sunk as a knee pressed into Elwood's back, surprising him out of his ecstatic adventure.

He stammered, "What? Huh?" Looking back over his shoulder, he tried to understand what was happening.

When the noose was slung over her lover's head, Laura knew all too well what was coming next.

Helping was the only thing she could do now. She had no idea why this was happening. Whatever the plan, someone else was in control. She was a marionette, and when her strings were pulled, Laura knew she had to dance to whatever tune played. Her job now was to push up on Elwood's shoulders so his head was in perfect position.

With the narrow leather strap tightening on his neck, and the knee digging into his back, Elwood looked at Laura with confusion and fear. The only plea he could manage was a guttural, "Ahhhhg." Though he tried, his hands were useless in trying to reach the constriction, being held back by the whore nestled under him. Her legs tightened around his waist to keep him still, choking him from the lower extremities, while the garrote crushed his larynx.

Squinting to increase her strength, her first thought to cooperate with Elwood's killer, but a pang of compassion waved through her, wishing this had just been another screw job and she could go home. Releasing his arms, his weight came down on the noose, making the end come faster. Stroking his bulging red face, she softly murmured the last words Ambassador Elwood Pierpont would ever hear. "I made you feel good and you were the best, honey. Thanks for dinner."

Laura was thankful he at least he got laid first, and she was thankful there was no blood. His legs quit thrashing and the body stilled, going limp on top of her. Sliding the thong from his neck, the killer let Elwood's head fell to her shoulder, his gray eyes bulging, staring blankly at her. Dead.

She never liked looking into the eyes of a dead person. It was just too creepy. A moment ago, he was euphoric, satisfied. Now his death eyes were inches from her face, as if to quizzically ask, "Why?"

The bulk of his lifeless body weighed heavily on her, and she tried to push him off, but the killer held him in place, the knee still on the ambassador's back. Leaning over the dead man, right to Laura's ear, the voice said, "Don't ever forget that you helped kill him. If anything ever leaks about this I'll personally slit your pretty white throat. Got it?"

Frightened way beyond what she dared to let on, Laura did her best to convince the killer she was loyal. Her voice was strained under Elwood's massive weight, wheezing out, "You know I'm good. I've never crossed any of you people. Any shit you pulled has always been a secret with me. You know I've been true. I always have been. I never told anyone about the others. You know that."

The panic in Laura's voice was her guarantee that she was loyal.

The knee lifted, and she was told, "I just wanted to make sure. Get dressed. You have to get rid of him." As silently as the shadow had come into the room, it floated out.

Laura heard a murmuring of voices in the other room. Then a hulk of a man Laura had never seen before rushed in. In a flurry, he snapped, "Get dressed. We've got a lot to do." Not quick enough to respond, he shot out, "Now, you dumb bitch! Move it!"

The man stepped away, leaving Laura with the burden of rolling the dead man away. Intimidation with the threat of pain was the catalyst to keep Laura and the other girls under control. This was the pimp's job, but sending in an enforcer instead of Billy put this episode into a different and more dangerous game. Laura was never in doubt that Billy was in control of the girls. But what controlled him was even more frightening. She had met a couple of the bosses, but they preferred to remain anonymous, especially to the whores. She was okay with that. They held powers she didn't want to know about, and ran in social circles she could only enter as a tool for pleasure.

Glancing at the pathetic shape of her customer, she saw that his erection had ebbed with his life. His hairy, paunchy body, flaccid with death repulsed her. She had to look away from the staring eyes. The eyes always bothered her. She couldn't get away from the thought that they could still see her. In them she could almost see the threat of horrible revenge. She didn't mind touching his body, disgusting as it was, didn't mind the caresses she administered as part of the job. She could easily take any part of him in her hand or mouth without reservations. Nothing was off limits. She could sit in a bath tub and pretend to get excited over a john urinating on her. She could kneel in front of them and feign pleasure at the privilege of having semen drip down her face. Anything was acceptable except having to look into the eyes of a dead man. And she has lost count of the times she has had to do it.

She kept a pair of jeans, sneakers, and a tee shirt in her bag, so she wouldn't have to go home dressed in a slinky evening gown. Going on the street in the early morning dressed as a prostitute increased her chances of being picked up and raped by a stranger, or worse, spotted by the police. The little black dress, cut both low and high, gave way to informal wear, which tonight would allow her more ability to help.

Tossing her douche kit and make-up bag into the duffel, she left Elwood on the bed to see what else was in store for her.

Stepping quickly into the living room, she found the man looking at a brief case Elwood had brought in with him. He turned, giving Laura an uncomfortable glance. Concerned, she asked, "How do I get paid for this. I've never seen you before and don't know..."

He barked, "Fuck the money. You'll get paid. Don't sweat it. Just do what you're told."

"Where's Billy? He's always taken care of us."

His sudden backhand sent her to the floor. "Didn't you hear me? Do what your told and you'll be taken care of."

Holding her face to stem the pain, she climbed to her feet, rasping out, "Okay, now I understand. Keep my mouth shut and do what I'm told. Got it. Please don't hit me again. Okay?"

"Smart bitch. I was told you'd be all right. Get moving. We have to drag him down the back steps."

Billy, normally the pimp in charge, kept a set of permanent rooms located at the rear of the third floor in the ancient hotel, with the hallway lights intentionally dimmed. The living area of the set of three rooms was dully lit by two table lamps casting an eerie glow. An active brewery at one time, the building had been converted into a turn-of-the-century collection of antique shops, boutiques, a book store, and a first-class restaurant. Charming and family friendly, Billy had gone to extremes to conceal his frequent use of the rented room, and the business he conducted. Disclosure of his activities would not be tolerated, and Billy would be looking for new digs.

The whore and the killer worked Elwood off the bed onto a throw rug, exerting a great deal of effort. Laura understood she needed to do her part. Taking a breath as he clumped to the floor, she asked, "I've never seen you before. What's your name?"

Annoyed, he sarcastically answered, "Larry. Happy now?"

"Yeah, sure. Larry."

Not bothering to dress the ambassador, Larry and Laura slid Elwood down the back steps naked, using the throw rug as a sled. His body jostled and jiggled over the stairs—*bump, bump, bump*. Laura held his arms over his head to control any rolling while Larry stepped backwards to ease him down the three flights.

An unfamiliar black Cadillac was already parked at the loading dock, so Laura knew the ambassador's murder had been planned ahead of time. Heaving the body up and stuffing it into the trunk, left her and the stranger out of breath. He stood and suddenly looked back up towards the room. A chill ran through him when he realized he had made a major mistake. The case was still in the room. He barked, still panting, "Go back upstairs . . . and get the suitcase. I'm gonna dump him. I'll meet you back here in about . . . half an hour. Got that?"

Nodding and beginning to move back to the building, Laura had to know. She shouldn't, but she asked anyway, "Why did you waste him? He had money and he was good for more."

Larry just barked, "Shut your fucking mouth, bitch. Do what I said." He brought his arm back as a threat, making her flinch. "Don't question me. I know what I'm doing."

Cowering, she backed away, "Yeah, I know. Don't worry. I'll get it. I'll be waiting." She forced a nervous smile. She watched the Cadillac drive out of the loading area. Fear rolled through her, clouding her brain. She had this frozen vision of what might be in store for her when he got back. No matter how much she earned as the syndicate's most productive prostitute, she was a witness to a famous man's brutal murder. Hell, she even helped do it. If she were in charge, she knew it would be a huge risk to let her live.

Her legs could barely support her as she climbed three flights of stairs to the room. Stopping to expel the dinner Elwood had bought for her, she wiped her hand over the sour remains on her mouth. Then, in a flash, it all became clear to her. She had been the last person to be seen with the ambassador tonight. Exposed in a busy restaurant, laughing and making a spectacle, anyone could have taken a photo of them.

Elwood Pierpont was a gregarious man, making a spectacle of himself laughing with beautiful women hanging on his arm. It was no secret that he did these things, and his wife made no issue of it. He was rich and powerful and the arrangement seemed to work for them. With three successful appointments under his belt he had no concerns over public opinion. Entrenched in Minnesota politics, he was a shoe-in for a possible run for governor, or even senator.

But when his body was discovered, she'd be the one they'd go looking for. Not the large angry stranger or the shadow with the leather strap—her. She had been set up, fully aware of what was going to happen and helpless to stop it. Laura understood that any one of the girls was expendable, their lives useful only as tools for obedience. This had to be why Billy, her pimp, had not been involved. He'd been in on it. He was selling her out, keeping out of sight, possibly with an alibi. And the most chilling thought: she likely would be killed when Larry came back for the case. Double jeopardy. She knew who had killed Elwood.

There had to be a defining motive to eliminate a gold mine like Pierpont. Nothing came to her that made sense, until she got back to the room and looked into the small suitcase Elwood had guarded so zealously. Filled with folded pieces of paper with green scrolled designs emblazoned on the front, each had a serial number and a value. Bearer bonds. A quick estimation showed they could easily amount to millions.

Laura had been with Billy for several years and had lived this long because she knew how to react to him. And she gave him and his bosses what they wanted. However, like a caged prisoner, the idea of escape and freedom was always an option. With the bonds in the suitcase in front of her, that door of opportunity had just opened. Having enough money to leave had always been her first problem. The second was avoiding Billy's wrath. Foremost in her mind was the set up for Elwood's killing. The amount of money in the case defined just how expendable she was, and she had no doubt that she would be branded as Elwood's killer.

She held a fortune in her hands and the killer was gone, for a while. If she was going to do something, she needed to act quickly. Racing through the rooms, she had to eliminate any evidence that she had ever been there.
She wiped clean the glasses they used before she seduced him, as well as the bottle of bourbon. Tearing the sheets off the bed, she stuffed them into the laundry drop across the hall. Doorknobs, faucet handles, toilet levers, anything that could possibly hold a trace to her identity she wiped clean.

Not bothering to lock the door, she ran to the rear staircase to avoid being seen in the lobby. If the clerk saw her with the suitcase, she would become a connection to the dead man. Out the rear entrance then. At 2:00 a.m., the alley was deserted. No sign of the Cadillac, so she slithered away in the blackness of the Lake Superior shore line.

Stopping in a dark copse of elm trees, she had no doubt what she was doing was insane. She had acted on impulse, searching for a way out of a tough life and a scary situation, and now it was too late to turn back. Hands on her knees, she leaned forward to think. "What now? What's next, girl? The next step, what is it?"

Her only connection to safety now was her best friend and fellow hooker, Carrie. Stepping back into in the darkness of the trees, she took out her cell phone. Pausing a moment to catch her breath and steady herself, she dialed the number. After too many rings, an annoyed voice answered, "What?"

Breathless, she leveled her voice to a whisper, "Carrie, there's trouble. Are you still working?"

Carrie shifted from annoyed to irritated, hoarsely whispering, "Yes, I'm working. Why wouldn't I? This is an all-nighter. He's asleep though. You know better than to call me. What's the problem?"

"Something bad happened. I have to see you. Call me back when you're done."

Neither party said goodbye.

Straightening up, she shouldered her bag and gripped the valise tightly. Looking up and down Superior Street, she saw the Blue-and-White cab parked in front of the hotel. Quickly sliding in, she was halted by the driver, "Sorry, lady, I got a fare coming. Maybe you could share it."

Her voice louder than expected, she thrust a fifty dollar bill at him. "No, get me out of here, now."

Looking at the bill, he hesitated, "Geez, I'm not sure . . ."

Frantically looking out the back window, she handed him two more, yelling, "The Greyhound station. Now, goddamn it. Get the fuck out of here."

Stuffing the wads of bills in his shirt pocket, he dropped the shifter into gear and laid a strip of rubber. "You got it, toots. Greyhound, here we come."

A few minutes later the cab ground to a skidding halt in front of the bus station. Laura tossed a fourth fifty onto his lap. As she tore out the door without closing it, he called after her, "Thanks, lady. Good luck." Under his breath, as he stood by the cab closing the door, he muttered, "You're gonna need it, I think."

Rushing to the customer service counter, she bought a permanent key to locker number 112. The case stuffed in, it would stay there indefinitely if she didn't come back.

Chapter Four

On the way to dump Elwood's body, Larry made a quick stop to pick up a passenger. The rear door opened, then closed. The voice from behind asked, "You've got him? He's here?"

"Yeah, in the trunk. We'll get rid of him now, then go back and get the case from the girl."

The voice in the back seat bellowed, "What do you mean, go back and get the case? You left it with a *whore*? I told you to bring it with, you idiot."

Defensively tossing his arms up, he explained, "I had to get out of there fast, and it was like dragging a beluga down the steps, getting this guy outa there. She'll get pinned for waxing the ambassador like we planned. Don't worry, we'll get the case. She can be trusted."

Louder yet, "*Trusted*? She's a whore, for Christ sake. Get back there and get the goddamn case. Now!" Fuming, the passenger hissed, "Then waste her."

Not happy with that last remark, Larry flinched, and the Cadillac made a quick u-turn, returning to the Fitgers Hotel. "Don't park in front. I don't want to be seen."

"Yeah, sure." As Larry got out, he noted a group of people out front looking like they were waiting for a cab.

Minutes later, Larry's heavy body waddled back to the Cadillac, sliding in behind the steering wheel. Panting, to the rear seat, "She's gone. She stripped the room and took the case. Nobody saw her leave through the lobby. Now what do we do?"

A moment of ominous silence passed before the voice in the back seat spoke, deep and growling, "Your name is Larry, huh?"

Glancing into the rear view mirror, Larry knew he was in trouble. "Yeah, Larry."

"Well, Larry, you know there's a price to pay for stupidity, don't you?"

Before Larry could try to justify his mistake the sharp blade came across his throat, neat, clean, and deep. The passenger opened the rear door and disappeared into the darkness that crowded the shoreline of Lake Superior. In the front seat of the Cadillac, Larry worked futilely at stemming the flow of blood spurting from his throat.

• •

The reason Laura was able to generate five-hundred dollars just for a man to have sex with her was obvious. Her physical appearance was stunning, and she carried herself with a grace that radiated sensuous appeal. Her deep-brown eyes could take a man prisoner. Accented by long dark-brown hair that curved way past her shoulder blades, she had the shape of a teen-ager. Center-fold gorgeous. Once she took a man into her arms, he couldn't get enough. She was guaranteed a return visit. It was this gift of inspiring sensual beauty that was about to save her life.

Turning the key to the depot storage locker, her peripheral vision caught three uniformed sailors. She felt them ogle her. Waiting for a bus ride to Minneapolis, their plans changed when the fox in the tee shirt became more important. Her moves were subtle, but effective, enticing them to follow as she left the depot. The pick-up was an easy one for her. It would be a gratis job, with their protection as payment. Besides, they couldn't afford her anyway. In Laura's justification, her price was the difference between being a whore and an escort.

Standing outside the bus station waiting for the sailors to connect, her plan was to get them to book a motel in town, or someplace outside of the Duluth proper. Knowing she could never go back to her apartment, she would work her way out of Minnesota and never return.

Seeing the GI's at the entrance looking at her, the first step was in place. Now, for a coy look, or even a casually seductive approach. She had to get out of sight as fast as possible and worry about coming back for the valise later. However, the best laid plans didn't always go as planned. She quickly found out she had made a fatal error. Her escape all fell apart when Billy's Buick screeched to a stop in front of her. Bouncing up onto the sidewalk, it almost ran over her.

Her instinct was to run to the sailors and hope they would protect her, but before she could unfreeze her fear, the pimp was out and clinging to her arm, shaking her wildly. His fist came across her face, sending her to the pavement, and his foot slammed into her side. She doubled into the blow, yelling at him from the sidewalk, "Billy, no don't. Don't hurt me."

Ignoring the gathering crowd, he screamed, "Bitch, you thought you could fuck with me? Cabbies will talk for a price, doll, and yours gave you up for fifty bucks." To finish his retort he brought his foot into the side of her head, jarring her senseless. "Where is it, Laura? Where's the case? You have no idea what you've done." Standing over her, his face deep red, he waved his clenched fists. He was pissed, but beneath it all, he was scared to death.

Coming up to her knees she felt the blood trickling down her face. The sidewalk spun beneath her. She pleaded, "Please, Billy, don't. I can explain." Her bag had slipped from her shoulder, lying on the pavement.

All he had to do was look into her pocket and find the key, and her life would end, and she knew it wouldn't be swift or painless. She was going to suffer as nobody else ever had. She had watched him, even helped him, terrorize other girls, and with Billy, there was no mercy.

She was groping for her pocket to give the key to him, trying to find a reasonable excuse for hiding the case, but her mind was in a fog. She knew she was as good as dead, until something happened that changed everything. The three sailors she had hoped to trap had followed her outside. They had been eying the attractive woman, making plans to try to pick her up and spend the night at a cheap hotel nearby. Following Laura outside, they angrily watched their target being beaten up by a guy who was screaming obscenities at her.

Rushing to her, they yelled, "Hey, asshole, stop that." Two sailors collared Billy, throwing him against the Buick. They began pounding him. "How do you like that, prick? Not so good with someone who can fight back." As the largest sailor threw his weight into Billy's face, "You don't hit women. Understand that?" His beating continued until the pimp was sitting on the sidewalk, cowering.

The third man had helped Laura to her feet, holding his handkerchief to the wound on her temple. "You all right, ma'am? Don't worry, he won't hurt you again."

He supported her while leading her to a bench to sit down. The commotion got worse when a police car pulled up with two officers stepping to Billy's aid.

"Back off, sailor, or you're going down." One of the cops knelt in front of Billy, assessing his condition. "Sir, can you talk to me?" The second officer held the sailors at bay. The third man rushed to his buddies, trying to explain their intervention. "He was beating and kicking that woman, sir. We had to stop it. He would have killed her."

Looking up, the officer asked, "What woman?"

Pointing to the bench, he said, "That one . . . ," but the bench was empty.

Getting back to Billy the cop said, "Sir, we're calling an ambulance for you."

Struggling to his feet, Billy stammered, "No, no ambulance. I'm okay. It was just a misunderstanding." Looking frantically around, he asked, "Where'd she go? The woman, where is she?"

The large GI pointed his finger at Billy, snarling, "You don't need to know, ass hole."

•••••••••••••••••••••••••••••••

Three-thirty in the morning, and the only refuge Laura had was a small coffee shop about a mile from the bus station, in a decrepit and dirty part of town. Nestled in a booth at the back, she ordered coffee and waited. Panic on a higher level set in when she discovered all her money and ID was in her bag, and it was lying on the sidewalk in front of the bus station. Worse, her cell phone was in the bag.

However, in truth, her bag was on Billy's lap, in his Buick. Rummaging through it, there was nothing he could use to find her. He was in front of her apartment waiting, a 9-mm pistol nestled under his leg. The silencer made it bulkier than he liked, but it was a necessary addition. To do what he planned, he would need a lot of time without being discovered. "That bitch is going to suffer." Also on his mind, was the repercussion he was going to endure for allowing this to happen. If he were to show up without the case of bonds, his own life would be worthless. After he received the frantic call, he rushed to the hotel and had seen what had happened to Larry. Since this whole setup was up to Billy to orchestrate, his life was over if he didn't recover the case of bonds.

The muted noise from the cell phone startled him. Fishing it out of Laura's bag, he pressed the answer button. From the other end, Carrie babbled, "Laura, what was so important? Laura? Come on, answer me."

Billy closed the phone without answering. He knew exactly where to go next.

Chapter Five

SITTING IN THE DESERTED COFFEE SHOP, Laura kept her back to the door, not wanting to see if Billy should happen to barge in looking for her. It was total denial on her part, but her fear had put a strangle hold on common sense. Going home was out of the question. He would have her apartment staked out while he cruised the streets looking for her. She couldn't trust Carrie or any of the other girls to hide her. It was too dangerous. No doubt they would sell her out to escape his wrath. If he caught her, there was absolutely nothing she could do to save herself. The intervention by the Navy had momentarily saved her life, but that probably only make Billy angrier.

Her head cradled in her hand, she moaned, "Oh, man, I'm fucked. What am I going to do?"

At this time of night, the restaurant was empty, except for Laura, who had become a problem for the waitress. Stopping by a couple of times to inquire, the gravel voiced woman asked, "You ready to order now?"

With a plea for a little understanding, all Laura could do was look mournful and shake her head. Shuffling away with a grumble, the waitress said, "You ain't gonna sit here forever, toots."

The front door made a small noise as it was opened, sending Laura's nervous system in orbit. Expecting an assault from Billy, she was startled when a man took the next booth. Her first reaction was that she had been discovered, but it was only an ordinary man in a wrinkled suit. He glanced at her and smiled but offered nothing more than a nod before picking up the menu. Occasionally, he would glance back at her, but she knew she was just an attraction to him.

Laura's use of the restaurant as a refuge ended abruptly. In a sarcastic rasping monotone, the waitress confronted Laura. "Look, honey, you've been sitting here too long already. Either order something or pay for the six gallons of coffee you drank and get the hell out of here. If you stiff me for it, I gotta pay, and I ain't gonna do that."

Looking up, Laura painfully told the waitress, "I can't pay. I don't have any money. Please don't make me leave."

The tears rolling down her face tugged at the waitress' compassion, but she pressed on. She had to. Her continued employment demanded it. "Look, honey, I don't want no trouble. I don't give a shit if you drink free coffee, but my boss does. If you don't pay, I have to, and you may think I'm Ivana Trump, but I ain't. I just look like her."

A heavyset man in a traditional greasy white cook's suit pushed the waitress aside. He leaned over Laura, on the borderline of yelling, "Pay up and get the hell out of here. We ain't no charity kitchen."

Words caught in her throat. Finally, she croaked, "I can't. Please."

Reaching to grab her arm, he gruffly said, "Come on. Get out now."

Laura, on the verge of hysteria, begged as she was hauled up from the seat, "Please, no, I can't go out there. He'll kill me."

Half way out of the booth with her feet dragging, the man in the next booth stepped in. "Hold up. She's with me." He sat down opposite Laura and handed the cook a twenty-dollar bill. "Here, take this and get your hands off her." He motioned the stunned woman back into the seat. He asked, "Have you eaten anything?"

Stammering, she said, "No," slowly lowering herself to the seat. The look on her face was between total fear and total confusion, but Laura's quick wits told her her situation had just flopped closer to salvation.

The man looked up at the cook, telling him, "Give her my order and make me another one."

Fingering the twenty, the cook asked, "You sure you want to get mixed up here?"

Irritated now, the man said, "Don't forget the onions. Go on. Hurry. I'm hungry."

"Suit yourself, Mac."

A moment later, the waitress set a plate in front of Laura. The stranger asked, "Do you want milk or coffee?"

Bewildered, and unsure of what she wanted, the man answered for her, "Bring us some milk."

The waitress shrugged, and walked away muttering, "Where are people like you when *I* need help?"

With her mouth hanging open in surprise, Laura looked at the man trying to find a reason for what just happened. From his appearance, she could guess his initial goal was to pick her up. Under the circumstances, that was what she needed most right now, and it was time to play his strings.

Munching his way through his own hamburger a few minutes later, the man watched the woman ravenously tear her way through a third-pound Jumbo Burger, and Joe's world-famous fries. Pushing back from the table, her fist covered a small burp. "I'm sorry." With a thankful, yet defiant look, she told him, "I can't pay you for this."

Smiling, he answered, "I didn't ask you to."

Nodding her head towards the kitchen, she said, "The cook might be right, you know. Are you sure you want to get mixed up with me?"

Smiling, the man put his hand on hers, "You don't look so dangerous. What kind of trouble are you in?"

Returning his contact with her fingers wrapped around his, she lied, "My husband beat me up. I had to get away."

He looked at the damage on the side of her face, "Did he do that?"

Her only response was a sad nod.

"Son of a bitch. I don't understand why some guys have to do things like that."

"You seem like a nice guy. Are you married?" She knew he was, but the question put more legitimacy on their conversation.

He fingered his ring, almost apologetically saying, "Yeah, I am."

"Well, she's a lucky woman to have you." Breaking an awkward pause, she added, "Where are you headed from here?"

"Minneapolis. I was at the Machine Tool Show for the company I work for. I'm an engineer. I was trying to find the freeway when I spotted this place and thought I'd better eat before I got on the road. I thought if I drove the rest of the night I could get home in pretty good time."

This unfortunate man, her knight in shining armor, was her ticket to freedom. Now she had to coerce him into helping her, possibly risking his life to do it. Her fingers started moving on his hand, softly massaging his mind. With a childish plea on her face, she bored her dark-brown eyes into his, saying, "You've done so much for me already, but I need to ask you for another favor."

Smiling, happy to have the attention of this beautiful woman, he blabbered, "Yeah, sure, anything."

"I need a ride."

"All right, where to?"

With the warmth and softness of her hand covering his, he would have agreed to anything. However, all she asked was, "To the bus depot?"

He was just an average guy with a geeky look and a wedding band. He had tousled reddish-brown hair and a nose that could have been smaller and still done the same job. Laura sized him up as an honest man, but one filled with frustration and unfilled fantasies, like so many other men deprived of the amazing sex they had only on their wedding night. Then when the relationship reached the *old stuff* level and the wife had a family to take care of, people like Laura stepped in to take care of their wants and needs. All she had to do to capture the man was to look at him, then with a gentle and personal touch, he would become Play-Doh to be molded as she wanted.

He paid the bill and left a tip. As he escorted her outside, he gently held her elbow—programmed respect for women. He held the door for her. The cook and waitress had watched the spectacle. The cook breathed, "Man, she's good."

Hesitating at the door, Laura clung to him, fearfully looking up and down the street.

He sensed her trepidation. "It's okay. I'm just parked over there. Come on."

Safely ensconced in his car, Laura slid down in the seat and directed him to the Greyhound Depot. Turning to her, he asked, "If you don't have any money how are you going to get on the bus?"

Gazing into her lap, she pulled her face up to look deep into his eyes, telling him, "I'm not taking the bus. There's something I need you to get for me." She handed him the key, "If my husband's looking for me, I don't want to be exposed in the station. Would you do it for me?"

Cautiously taking the key, he said, "I'm not going to get in trouble am I? I don't want to get between you and your husband."

"Don't worry. He doesn't know you." As a clincher to get him motivated, she put her hand on his leg, and softly caressed him. "Please."

Mesmerized, he would let her poop in his pocket if she wanted to. Gorgeous beyond belief, Laura was sitting close to him, crawling her way into his mind, rubbing his leg.

Holding the key up to the light, he stammered, "Number 112. I'll be right back." He instinctively reached for the ignition key, but pulled back. Taking it would tell her that he didn't trust her, and he didn't want to hurt her feelings. They traded smiles and he got out.

She was well aware of his hesitance at taking the key. It was her job to notice the small moves. It told her what he was all about. Mid-western ignorance and character. Another frustrated and helpless man, trying to satisfy an implied image of being a good person. Don't offend and give everyone what they expected. Be respectful and polite, at any cost to his feelings. Laura had earned a fortune for Billy and his bosses catering to dopes like this. She would wind herself around his libido, rendering him helpless, dangling over the side of the boat, to be devoured when she wanted.

Returning to the car, she was alarmed to see the careless way he held the precious case, nearly holding it aloft. She wished he would at least tuck it under his arm. Sliding into the driver's seat, he asked, "What's so important in this thing?"

She reached eagerly for it even as she tried to minimize its importance. "Just some papers to show my lawyer about the abuse from my husband. I have to divorce him before he hurts me anymore." She set the case on the floor between her feet even though her inclination would have been to clutch it to her chest.

His homespun concern was not going to let her be exposed to danger, or an abusive husband. He asked, "Now what do we do with you? I don't want to leave you someplace where you're going to get beaten again. Don't you have someplace to go?"

Now, Laura was on stage, and she knew she had to win her Oscar. Feigning a sadness that filled the man's face with pity, she asked, "Is there any chance you could get me out of Duluth? If I go home he'll kill me."

He carefully reached over, lightly touching the dried blood on her face, saying, "Nobody should ever do that to a woman. Yeah, I'll take you as far as you want to go. Do you have relatives or friends you can stay with?"

"No, I don't have anybody except a sister, but I could never barge in on her. The first thing she'd do would be to call my husband. My parents are gone. There's no one else. I'm alone, no kids, and being afraid of my husband, well . . . no, there's nobody." She didn't dare look at him, afraid he might see the theatrics in her eyes. She kept her gaze on her lap.

His empathy for her pathetic situation overwhelmed him. There was only one alternative. He quietly said, "I could take you with me, but I'm married."

She put her hand back on his leg, telling him, "Oh, no. I wouldn't want to cause any problems for you. Maybe you could let me off at one of the truck stops."

Concerned, he wrinkled his brow, "Well, then what?"

"I don't know. I just can't stay around here. Please?"

"Sure, I could do that." Uncomfortable with the prospect of abandoning her, he said, "I don't want any trouble. I'm married, you know, and I don't think my wife would understand my being with you for any reason."

Letting her slow smile melt into him, she said, "I wouldn't let that happen to you, I owe you so much. My own marriage is in a shambles. I wouldn't want to ruin yours."

As if mounting his white stallion, her savior in shining armor boasted, "I'm definitely not going to leave you in a truck stop, or abandoned in a gas station. I have an idea. Direct me to the freeway and show me which way to Minneapolis."

The threaded drive through Duluth to the highway was compounded by permanent construction, which in the dark was a maze of lane changing and a lot of luck to avoid an erroneous exit or collision with another confused driver.

Enveloped by the tangle of orange cones, detour signs, and barriers, Laura guided him to the hill that exited Duluth and became I-35. Accelerating onto the right-hand lane, he smiled and said, "Thanks. I wonder if they'll ever finish fixing this road. I would've gotten lost for sure without you."

Turning to face him, her voice was quiet, "No problem. I don't even know your name. Maybe we should introduce ourselves."

Sporting a silly crooked grin, he told her, "Oh, I'm sorry. I'm Donald. Don Portman."

Reaching out, she softly purred, "Hi, Don. I'm Laura Blake. I really appreciate your help. Thanks." The ensuing silence became heavy, so she started a general conversation. "You said you had an idea. A good one?"

Proud of being so resourceful, he told her, "There's a little town, rather a spot in the road, called Carlton. It's about twenty minutes ahead. There's a casino on this side of the freeway with a hotel. I've never stayed there, but its all lit up and looks like a decent place. I was thinking we could, um, maybe . . ."

Forcing a light chuckle, she touched his arm, "I'll make it easy for you, Don. You're trying to ask me if I'd stay there with you—right?"

With a guffaw that could have come from a pubescent boy, he confessed, "Yeah, I was, but didn't dare be too . . . you know."

"Yes, I do know, Don. And don't worry about offending me. I'm a big girl." Not wanting to lose control of the conversation, Laura kept talking. "Tell me about your wife. What's she like?" Ignoring the seat belt law, her legs were up on the seat so she could twist herself closer.

"Melanie? Just a wife, nothing special. She keeps busy with three kids and a house."

"Describe her for me." Now she could worm her way into the corner of his mind that all married men had. The distant wife who found everything important except her husband's sex life.

"She's put on a little weight after three kids. We don't talk much, except about what a rough day she's had. I guess it's a typical marriage."

"That doesn't sound typical, or happy. Some women lose their husbands when they stop having sex with them. That's so wrong."

Surprised that the conversation would turn to this, Don jumped at a chance to talk openly. Especially to such a beautiful woman who thought sex should be a part of marriage. "You really think so? How about you and your husband? Do you . . . you know, do you . . . ?"

She saved his ego by finishing his question. "Do my husband and I have sex? Not nearly as much as I want to. Since he's taken to violence, I avoid him and I miss being in bed with a man." Now for her stellar performance, in a deep dreamy tone, she added, "What I wouldn't give for a man who just wanted to make love to me."

The Buick almost left the road as Don gasped, "Are you serious?"

"Yes, I am, Don, and for what you've done for me, I'd love to do it with you. You are the nicest man I've ever met, and frankly, honey, you're turning me on. Just imagine how good it would be to know your wife will never find out. Just the two of us laying naked, doing what we both so desperately want." To seal the deal, her fingers caressed the back of his neck, sending the poor man into orbit.

The only reaction he could manage was a breathless, "Oh, my. Really?"

As the highway rolled under the car, she kept his interest, and his erection, on her and what was waiting for him. Casual comments with some chuckles, his imagination was running away, wishing that she was his wife. It was so easy to talk to her and get her interest in anything he said, as if they had known each other for years. Laura Blake, actress, seductress, Don Portman's wife or prostitute, whatever it took to get what she needed.

Laura put her hands to her mouth to give the look of appreciation, and also to hide her mirth at what he was trying to do. *Keep this sap on a string and I'll do just fine.* "Of course, Don. I owe you so much."

His mind doing somersaults, he tried to sound casual. "What do you do when you aren't in trouble?"

"I'm a model. Magazines, tooth paste ads, whatever they wanted."

Turning to her, he was compelled to say the obvious, "Well, it's no surprise that you're a model. You're a very beautiful woman." He colored to his scalp. "I'm sorry. I didn't mean to be forward."

Shifting closer, she pulled the marionette strings a little tighter. "A girl never gets tired of a compliment, Don. Thank you. However, this has been so ... damaging, getting beat up like this. I don't think I'll be able to work for a long time and I don't know how I'll get by."

Pulling up to the hotel entrance, he shut down the car and looked at her. "Well, let's go in."

Laura knew that if she approached the reception desk, she might likely be recognized as a regular with a john. Hesitating, she asked, "Would you mind if I wait in the car while you register? I'm . . . I don't want to attract attention with my face all banged up."

He gave her a longing look. "You're beautiful no matter what. Wait here." He marched off like a hero saving a princess.

However, her thought was more realistic . . . *you dumb shit.*

There was no hesitation with the keys this time, and Laura knew she could leave without him. But, he was the one with available cash, and a credit card. She couldn't afford to be made by the Highway Patrol looking for his stolen car.

Soon, he came skipping back to the car, a joyous smile beaming across his face. "We're on the ground floor half way down the hall. There's nobody at the desk now, so if we go in quick you can keep your head down. You can walk on the other side of me and keep hidden. Nobody will see your face."

Apprehensive, Laura nodded and slid out, clenching the briefcase. Her head down, they hurried through the lobby, but didn't go unnoticed. Trained to watch the traffic, the clerk eyed the woman, commenting to himself, "Hmm, again?" At one time, the clerk had propositioned Laura himself, but she'd blown him off thinking it would just lead to trouble with Billy.

At the door to the room, Don asked again, "Are you sure this is all right?"

"It's perfect for me, Don. Are you afraid?"

He confessed, "Yeah, a little." Then as a truthful afterthought, "A lot. I've never done this since I got married, and not even much before that."

Leaning into him, she softly said, "Nobody will ever know. I probably want this more than you do. I'm married also, Don. If my husband found out he'd kill me. This will be our own time together. Just you and me."

Looking over the room, she knew he'd popped for a more expensive suite to impress her. "This is awesome, Don." Setting the case down, she sat down at the edge of the bed, drew him down to sit with her and put her arms around his neck. She kissed him, full and firm. In a moment, they were reclining across the spread. She was aware of his wanting to feel her, so she opened the doors of permission, placing one of his hands on her rear, and the other on her breast.

One of her hands held his head still for her tongue to work on his, while the other dropped to his zipper.

He was primed, so she needed him to relax and get his responsibility out of the way. "You should call your wife," she whispered seductively, "let her know you're on the way. Don't let her worry."

Reluctantly, he placed the call. He improvised that there'd been some last-minute meetings he needed to attend. He would be gone another night. When he mumbled, "Yeah, me too," into the phone, Laura let him see her smile and approve.

When the call was completed, she crawled across the bed, telling him, "Always tell her you love her, Don. It'll make her feel good." Then, to justify the affair they were about to embark on, she said, "What we're going to do is different, you know. Don't feel guilty about it. It's only to release some tight feelings and feel good. And, I want to more than you know."

He rolled over to caress her warm soft body that was letting him satisfy every fantasy he has ever had, plus a few of Laura's. In her game to capture this man and hold onto the safety he could offer her, she was astounded when she reached a climax. She couldn't recall the last time she had made love to a man when Billy wasn't waiting for his cut. Maybe more important was that this poor dope had no idea he was a john. He was in this for real. This was so different from orchestrated animations to make money for a man who knew she was a whore and for a man who would beat her silly on a whim.

Rolling on top of him, she told him the first thing that was not a lie or overt manipulation. Running her fingers along his face, she kissed him gently. "Don, it's been so long since I felt like this with anyone. I hardly know you, yet I'm feeling a connection to you that's so close and warm."

Not wanting to lose this moment, Don pleaded, "Laura, will you come to Minneapolis with me? We'll find a place for you to stay. We can be together."

This was starting to sound like a soap opera. She needed to set some limits, yet it was important that he get her further away from Duluth. "Don, I think the world of you, and you probably saved my life tonight, but I'm not going to become the reason for a family breaking up. Can we just get there and see how it goes?"

Not in the least deterred, Don grinned. Rolling off the bed, he announced another fantasy he had. "Let's take a shower together."

"Okay, but do you mind if I call my sister while you get it going? We're terribly close and she's going to worry if I don't get hold of her."

He tossed her the cell phone, and then danced delightedly into the bathroom.

Making sure Don was busy in the bathroom, she punched the numbers. The phone was answered immediately. "Carrie, can you talk?"

"Laura! Yes! Where are you?"

"I'm in trouble Carrie. You're the only person I can trust. Please don't sell me out to Billy."

Laura's panic caused her to miss Carrie's hesitation. "Don't worry, honey, I won't tell him. Where are you?"

"I picked up some guy near the bus depot and he got me out of town. I had to get away or Billy would've killed me. Are you okay?"

"I'm fine, but what are you going to do?"

"He's taking me to Minneapolis. He has family there. I think I can get him to put up me up for a while. Carrie, can you come with me? You should get out of there before you get killed. Please, honey, meet me in Minneapolis."

There was an uncomfortable pause, until Carrie nervously answered, "Sure, Laura. Yeah, I'll meet you there. Do you still have your phone?"

Carrie's question didn't seem to make sense. "No, I lost it when Billy caught me."

Carrie told her, "It doesn't matter. Where are you now?"

Laura heard the bathroom door open. Don stood there, wet and naked, waiting for her. "I gotta go. I'll call you in the morning." With that, Laura joined Don in the shower.

Back in Duluth, in Carrie's apartment, Billy took the phone from her. Smiling, he said, "That was perfect, Carrie. Thank you. I won't forget it. Now, we wait for her to get hold of you in the morning."

Chapter Six

Still in my office, I put the pictures of Marci and Cheryl in safe place and thought about building an altar to display them with reverence. Angry at my own wishy-washy attitude, I had to get out of there. This office was more Jeanine's than mine, and if she needed me I'd come back. Maybe she could find Elwood Pierpont. In my misery I decided I didn't give a shit if he ever showed up. I just didn't want to give the money back. Dragging myself out of the office, I slowly drove home, hoping I didn't forget to buy some booze.

This time of night and at this end of Superior Street reminded me of a movie set with monsters and zombies walking stiff legged looking for humans to eat. Dark, vacant, and dead quiet, the only sound came from the trendy Canal Park district, not far away. With the blighted economy, even that showpiece was low on business.

Trying to convince myself that I needed to hoist my body up two flights of stairs, before the zombies got me, I was scared shitless by the sudden appearance of a dark figure standing next to me. My gun was out before my heart started pumping again.

Tall, draped in a black wool overcoat, the grizzled head of Homer the Hanky sat at the top of the apparition. "Jesus, Hanky, you can't be creeping up on old fat men like that. My heart's going into orbit now." Clutching my chest, I leaned over and patted his arm to let him know he was in good stead with me. I hoped he didn't notice the pistol I was holding. Recovering, I asked, "What's up, Hanky. You usually don't usually show up like this. You okay?"

Maybe Hanky really was a zombie. He stared at me with his sunken eyes and bony face, looking as creepy as any zombie should look. The crop of gray bristles covering his jowls looked like a thistle bush, and as he slowly spoke, I could see there was something he didn't like. This decrepit recuse lived in the bowls of darkness avoiding any form of human connection. He and I got close when I stumbled upon him getting his ass kicked by a gang of street lords looking for a kill. I got my own ass wiped in trying to shoo them away, but I hurt them enough so they never came back.

His voice had the same sound as rocks going through a grinder—low, hoarse, and garbled. He pointed a bony finger behind him, saying, "I hear things. Bad news travels fast. I hear it. Bad guy. Back there."

I looked back to where he was pointing and started thinking how I could convince him I didn't know what the hell he was talking about. But, Homer never spoke unless there was something to say that was more important than not talking. The man was still human, but he had some mysterious ways about him. When he said *Bad guy. Back there,* wasn't just gab to spin a conversation out of me. He was nervous and obviously knew something had happened that shouldn't have.

Quietly, with assurance that I believed him, I asked, "What bad guy, Homer?"

His breath came in spurts. I knew he was scared. "By the hotel. Cops all over."

My hand on his bony shoulder, I asked, "Is someone dead, Homer?"

"Dead guy. By the hotel."

He knew I was his friend and would never betray him, so I bluntly asked, "Did you have anything to do with it, Homer?"

Backing up, his hands pushing me away, "No, not me. No."

"I believe you, Homer. Is there anything there that could point to you? Did you leave anything there?"

"I leave nothing. All in here." He patted his long coat which must have been full of pockets with secret stashes.

"You can hide in my apartment if you want. I don't want the cops to find you anywhere near there. You'd be their first arrest." My inner fear was that if someone was dead as he said, maybe Hanky was the killer.

Without a word Hanky glided away down Superior Street, and I knew I wouldn't see him again until the danger was passed. Before he left I slipped him three tens in case he was out of hooch. I knew it would never go for food. Looking up the street, the Fitgers Hotel wasn't too far away. I owed it to Hanky to look into it.

From blocks away I could see the colorful attraction of flashing blue and red lights celebrating a crime scene. My Reliant dieseled to a stop outside the yellow tape barrier. The creaking driver's door announced my arrival. Out of courtesy, and because I wouldn't be allowed any closer on my own, I approached my nemesis, Detective Stu Grosslein. "Hey, Grossy, what's shakin'?" He ignored my outstretched hand.

He happily welcomed me, "Shit, what are you doing here?"

"I just can't stay away from a party, Grossy. Heard you had a body. I'm tingling to look at another dead guy."

"You heard there was a body? Tell me, Klein, how'd you hear so quick about there being a body? This has nothing to do with you. When guys like you show up uninvited, I get suspicious." Detective Grosslein stood too close to me, holding his little tablet poised, waiting for me to tell him what I knew. I wanted to laugh at the tiny stub of his pencil, but for once, I was smart enough to keep my humor to myself. Behind him, a series of flood lights had been set up, and the forensics crew was trying to map out the area and analyze what happened.

"Again, Grosslein . . ."

Correcting me, he hissed, "*Detective* Grosslein, if you don't mind. Now, tell me."

"Shit, Grossy, don't play that game with me. I don't need to be reminded of who you are and the 'detective' title sounds stupid when you want to feel important. Just take my statement and go to work."

I had pushed his professional exasperation to the limit and he railed on me. "Klein, don't lecture me. I want to make sure we get it all. You should know that better than anyone. Now, try being a stand-up citizen and tell me why you're here."

Sighing, I knew he was right, but had a problem giving in to him. Stu Grosslein and I had been friends since high school in South Minneapolis. We would cruise Lake Street and Broadway picking up girls, and testing various fake IDs to buy beer. Now, he was stuck in a low pay, no way job and wanted my cooperation. "Okay. I heard a rumor some shit was going on here and came to see."

He shoved his ridiculous prop and stubby pencil back into his pocket and I knew he wanted to talk about what happened here. Which meant that he hadn't a clue what went down, or why? By including me, he was grasping at anything to put into a logical report.

Acting like a cop, he led me to a black Cadillac parked in the dark, up the street. I assumed it had been dark at the time it was parked because no streetlamp stood nearby, but now the Caddy was under intense lighting from portable police flood lamps. The blood covering the front seat left nothing to the imagination. Hanky was correct, something bad had happened.

The trunk lid yawned open, and a couple of suits leaned in with portable floods. Evidently, what was in the trunk was more interesting than the bloody front seat. As I peered over the backs of the suits, I saw why. I recognized him. Elwood Pierpont was no longer missing. My shock seeped out just loud enough to be heard by every cop standing here. "Oh, shit, no. Not him."

The two suits at the trunk turned, eyeing me with disdain. Detective Grosslein suddenly grabbed me by my collar, and yelled into my face, "You *do* know something, Klein. Your dropping by here was no accident, was it? Okay, spill it. Tell me what's going on."

Slipping out of his grip, I wedged between the two offended cops, pointing at the fat nude crammed into the trunk. "That's Elwood Pierpont. His wife just hired me to find him."

Detective Grosslein, trying to sound professional, spouted, "Oh, yeah? There was no missing person out on him. Why would she hire someone like you to find him if he ain't missing?"

"Grossy, you offend my tender self with your accusation that I'm not worthy of the Pierponts' business. To ease your busy little mind, I was hired to see that his philandering didn't get into the newspapers." I remembered about the "thing" I also had to find. I thought that if the cops hadn't found the missing whatever, whoever killed him had it. That would be my secret, and a reason to revisit the Pierpont mansion—and the delectable Kathleen.

The questioning droned on for a few more minutes before Grossy decided he had fulfilled his obligation as a policeman. I agreed to stay in touch, and ended the evening with him by saying, "I'll be down to the station when I can, Grossy. I'd like to be in the loop with this."

As I lugged myself back to the Reliant, I heard his answer. "There ain't no loop, Klein. Stay out of the way."

● ●

Nursing a fine imported selection of rot-gut fire water, I sat alone in the dark of my apartment listening to the cockroaches fight with the mice for tidbits left lying around. "What was Elwood's body doing in the trunk of a Cadillac? Naked?" Well, it had been a Caddy. With the Pierpont status, I couldn't imagine him being stuffed into a Reliant, or lowly Chevy. But he hadn't been alone. Someone else had been killed in the front seat. "Who was that stiff?"

Adelle Pierpont was the only person who knew I was hired to find him. Well, there was also the babe with the nice ass, Kathleen. It took a nanosecond more to realize, "Elwood was expendable. He was obviously killed for the mystery item I was supposed to find. Whatever it was." I had a hunch that if Adelle Pierpont didn't have the whatever, I was still on the payroll to find it. If she did have it, did I care anyway? Not really.

The next morning came too soon, just like yesterday morning. Adelle Pierpont needed to answer a few questions, and I needed to look presentable to make a favorable impression on her. She already thought I was a desperate piece of shit willing to do anything for a price. How perceptive of her.

In case the fox was there, I at least thought I should wear a clean shirt. I didn't have one, but I knew how to get one. I grabbed a dirty shirt from the back of a chair and headed for the hall. I tapped on Mrs. Feldstein's door and waited. Listening to the rustling on the other side I knew she was arming herself. "Who's there? Speak up, I have a weapon in here and I'll use it."

Calling through the oak panels I said, "Mrs. Feldstein, it's Norby. It's okay."

I listened patiently as six chains were detached, and two deadbolts thunked out of the way. The door opened two inches, and an eyeball peered out. As soon as Mrs. Feldstein, all two and a half hundred pounds of her, recognized me and understood she was not going to be raped or sodomized, she opened the door wide.

Throwing her arms up, she got me in a bear hug that threatened my ribs. As she swooned and chortled with glee, about a dozen Spoolies popped from the short gray hair trying to cover her head. For lack of anything else to do, she made frequent trips to a salon for perms or haircuts. When there was no hair left, which didn't look too far in the future, she could have her scalp tattooed with pictures of Spoolies.

"Sorry to bother you, but..."

Her voice loud, happy, and bossy, "Bother, schmother, for you I always have time." In her telepathic and swift actions, she snatched the shirt out of my hands and pushed me into a kitchen chair. Within moments I was eating a heaping plate of orthodox something that smelled strongly of garlic. What was I doing? It was only ten in the morning? When I pushed back trying to keep from belching, I passed gas instead.

While she washed, dried, and ironed the shirt, even sewed a loose button into place, she kept up a lively conversation, never really noticing or caring if I took part. Incessantly on and on, her chatter was driving me to the edge, but I loved her for it. She was lonely and had adopted me. I would never forget the time she fished the bullet meant for Louie out of my shoulder and nursed me to the almost healthy man I was at present.

I couldn't get away until she had been allowed to give my pants the clean treatment as well. Sitting in my boxers, I crossed my legs to hide the rip in the crotch. I couldn't bear for her to insist on sewing that. The shirt was still warm from the iron when I shrugged it on, and I stood in place while she planted a big wet kiss on my mouth. She had no teeth.

•••••••••••••••••••••••••••••••••

This was only my second visit to the Pierpont castle, but the absence of obvious servants seemed unusual. Babe-amundo opened the door and gave me about twelve-seconds to ogle her. More casual this time, her legs and ass were covered by what I thought women called peddle pushers. Maybe Nordstrom's or Macy's called them Capri's. Whatever.

A sleeveless blouse tastefully unbuttoned to the bottom of her bra covered the rest of the statue. Today, her hair hung tangled and loose around her face, like she had been in the rack with some guy. My fantasy let me linger on the idea that she had left it unkempt just to entice me. It worked.

"Mr. Klein, we were expecting you." Her voice was as hot as her body.

Stammering, "Yeah, well, I thought I'd better see what's up."

Standing aside, she nodded her head as an invitation to enter the hallowed hall.

Today, her highness, Adelle Pierpont, sat on a patio I understood was called a veranda. A wrought- iron chair and a glass-topped table was her throne for today. So far, Kathleen was not asked to leave, but I hoped she would disappear so I could start acting like a grownup again.

Adelle's voice was no softer than before. "Mr. Klein, sit."

Feeling suddenly like an eager golden retriever, wagging my tail and panting, I obeyed. "Detective Grosslein told me you had been informed about Mr. Pierpont's death. I'm sorry." I looked for the cane, but it wasn't in view.

To the abrupt point, Adelle said, "Why are you sorry? You didn't know him."

My peripheral vision caught Kathleen grinning. I was being shoved through a Cuisinart and she thought it was funny. I thought it was time for me to be direct, although it might not be in my financial interest. "Now that he's been located, and I wasn't the one to find him, do you want your money back?"

"Don't be absurd, you aren't done yet. When you bring me the missing package I'll give you another check for the same amount."

I worked really hard to contain my surprise and greed. "Well, that's a start. At least I know this thing is a package. And I can guess by your concern, a valuable package. One more valuable than the death of your husband?"

She had no trouble hiding any emotional response. "Infinitely more valuable. My husband is dead and I don't give a shit. We'll bury the philandering bastard in a respectable show and get on with our lives. Yes, Mr. Klein, the *package,* as you say, is valuable. Look for a black leather valise, about a foot wide and a little longer. It'll have a clasp on it, but that's probably broken by now." She glanced at Kathleen, and then turned to me in a lower but still harsh voice, "They are bearer bonds, Mr. Klein. That's all you need to know."

She sat back and flicked her fingers at me as if I was an ash on a cigarette. "Now, go earn your money and bring it to me. All of it."

That was the signal for me to get out. Kathleen stood and motioned towards the door, confirmation I was getting kicked out. Following her ass to the front door, I asked her, "I've never been kicked out of places better than this, but maybe I can convince you to tell me more about what this is all about. Would you? Could you?"

She leaned on the edge of the open door, sizing me up. I had done that to her, and I hoped I hadn't made her as uncomfortable as I was now. When her gaze had traveled up my body, it landed on my eyes, and I could swear she was hypnotizing me. It was working. She's going to turn me into a toad, I can feel it.

Her lips parted, the lids on those marvelous pools of deep-brown closed slightly, and she said, "What can I tell you?"

How the hell do I know? Regaining my composure, a little bit, I fumbled with the words, "I don't know." That small exchange of nonsense made me feel like garbage, and her answer stunned me.

"Meet me in the Midi Lounge in Fitgers at eleven."

I wasn't aware of stepping through the doorway, but looking back I saw her watching me. She still had me captured her in her gaze until the large heavy door slowly shut.

Fitgers was an enigma of many facets. Originally a brewery, it was a quaint and comfortable turn-of-the-century brick building housing a few restaurants, a book store, gift shops, and a nostalgic display of a copper brew vat. A wonder display of class and charm. The Midi Lounge was a moderately up-scale place where a couple could relax and share a good meal. Just down the street was where the ambassador had been found.

I tried to arrive on time, but my nature just wasn't an 'on time' element. There weren't too many people, and I had no trouble spotting her as soon as I stepped inside. I made an effort to be nonchalant as I stumbled across the floor, tripping on my own feet.

She acknowledged me by glancing at me and returning to her drink. Clad in a satin crème-colored sleeveless dress, she looked like royalty. The hem of the almost-too-short dress sported a three-inch fringe that I could imagine being drawn over my face. The pearls wrapped loosely around her neck were more valuable than the retainer check her mother had given me.

She spoke to me through the mist of my delusion that I was good enough to be on the same planet with her. "Mr. Klein, good of you to show up. You looked like a bourbon man, so I ordered one for you."

She stood up and teetered slightly, "Oops, silly me, I'm drunk. Grab your drink and we can go upstairs. I have a room waiting."

Her highness glided out of the dining room, leaving her shoes under the table. Confused as a kid in a calculus test, I balanced the bourbon while fetching her shoes. If I hadn't gotten to the elevator in time, I was certain she would have gone up without me. If I had any common sense I'd have let her go. But you know how that goes.

Standing beside her in the elevator I could feel the heat emanating from her body, and it didn't smell like Right Guard. "Oh, my shoes. How good of you."

Stopping on the top floor, she managed to make it to the room she wanted still standing up. Having no idea what to expect, I entered the room with hesitation, until she cleared the doubt. "Be a dear and fix me a drink. I'll have what you have." She headed for the bathroom, neglecting to shut the door.

A fully stocked bar with normal sized bottles and not the typical mini-bar minis was built into the wall. It even had tap beer. Not being a beer occasion, I experimented with a unique crème sherry. Combined with the bourbon I could look forward to a king size headache and my face buried in the toilet. Speaking of toilets, I heard one flush through the open bathroom door.

As her highness had a manner of floating, rather than making walking sounds, she scared the crap out of me when she reached from behind to take possession of her drink.

She was naked.

Downing the juice in one gulp, she picked up a bottle of Courvoisier from the bar while chastising me, "This is not a wine night, honey. Get undressed."

I tried to pry a thought out of my brain that, technically, cognac was considered a wine family member, but it was too processed. Following her floating to the bedroom, I looked like a bicycle with the kickstand down—or up. I don't know. Whatever God did in creating this woman he out-did Himself. Just watching her flesh move in a poetic flow of seduction and art took my breath away. I quickly blew into my hand to see if said breath was tainted. She was absolute perfection, but a confirmed lush with an obvious sexual appetite meant for King-Kong. To consider having sex with me, it had to be nothing more than satisfying a narcotic need to fuck. I was game.

I won't go into details about what happened in the bedroom. I was in a daze most of the time. Waking up and believing it was daytime, I tried sitting up without barfing all over the now wet and rumpled satin sheets. The space on the bed next to me was empty. The distant sound of voices and a door closing put my mind on alert, but my body was not ready for it.

Kathleen sashayed into the bedroom with a tray of coffee that sent an aroma of salvation to me. Setting it on the table, she turned to me and must have encoded the question on my face, "Room service. Now, what was it you wanted to talk about?" Beige must be her signature color, as the beige satin wrap she wore just slid off her body.

"Aw, Jesus, Kathleen, how can I talk when you do that to me? Do you have to be naked?"

Now she came out to play. Crawling across the bed like a panther in heat, she hissed, "Don't you like it?"

As I scanned her body again, I was amazed, and highly pleased, that she must have bathed in a depilatory. Her nudity was the only obstacle between me and the coffee, so I pulled her down and did it all over again. With that out of the way, it was an open field to the carafe of caffeine. Convincing her that I could speak more fluently if she was covered, she obliged by draping the flimsy bed wrap over her breasts. "Okay, fussy, what do you want to know?"

My answer didn't faze her a bit. "Other than wanting to know if you are a good fuck, I can't remember. Oh, yeah, tell me about your father, Elwood."

Her hesitation and the stiffening of her lips told me more than she was going to. "Elwood. My goddamn father, good old Elwood. He was a bastard. That's about it."

"Tell me about your mother."

Her response was quick and curt. "The ice queen. I was an only child and never knew the bastard or the ice queen until I was old enough to realize I didn't know who my parents were. By the time I was eighteen, I had made enough trouble for them to get me shipped out to Sweden for an education. Convenient and it shut me up."

Impressed, I reiterated, "Sweden, how nice."

Scorn dripped from her lips. "Not really. I'd been there before, forced to go when I was twelve. Not a pleasant trip."

"Plenty of kids have an unhappy childhood. Yours just happened to be on a higher level. What do you know about these missing bonds that have your mother all choked up?"

If I wasn't so enamored with her nakedness I could have possibly caught a nanosecond hesitation in her demeanor.

Lying back, the flimsy bed wrap stayed in place, while her arms waved away the importance of the topic. "I don't get involved in all that. I leave the money stuff to Adelle. I get an allowance to blow on frivolities like you."

I'd been classified as a frivolity, which was far better than the usual term of asshole to describe me. Continuing, my next question brought our interlude to an end. "Who would want Elwood dead?"

She looked at me and laughed. A pathetic chortle belied by a mist collecting in her eyes. "What kind of detective are you? *Everyone* wanted him dead. The bonds were just a good reason to do it."

The beautiful and unpredictable Kathleen Pierpont abruptly ended our romance by picking up her slinky dress and walking out of the room. Turning at the door, she told me, "I wanted him dead. We all did." She dressed, and I listened to the door of the hotel room open and close, and sat absorbing the deadness of the love chamber.

Still no closer to the bonds, at least I knew why he was killed. Someday, I'll find out who did it.

CHAPTER SEVEN

DETECTIVE STU GROSSLEIN WELCOMED ME into his cubical with a greeting that gave a wad of gum on his shoe more status. "Oh, Christ, Klein, what the hell do you want?"

I captured his coffee cup, but put it back when I saw the cigarette butt floating in it. "Sheeze, you drink that?"

Smiling, he retorted, "It kept you away. Whadda ya want? Tell me quick and get out of here."

"I want to know what you found on the ambassador."

"You ain't a cop, Klein. Go away."

I hoped my next comment would make him more agreeable. "The ambassador's wife hired me to find him and bring him home." I was right, Grossy became interested.

"Yeah, that's what you said last night. Why would she hire you? I've already talked to her, and her gardener looks better than you. Fill me in, Klein."

Mocking him, I repeated, "*Fill me in, Klein.* I asked what you found on the Ambassador. You want fill, and I want answers."

He was interested but couldn't bring himself to be nice to me. "I told you, you ain't a cop. And, dipshit, if you are withholding evidence, I'll make you a resident in our hotel here."

"You're getting nowhere here, Grossy. Let me work with you, and we can close this thing by the end of the day."

"The only thing I'll close is your mouth." He hesitated, calmed down and slowly asked, "What you got?"

That's the way it was between us. Our relationship hinged on brutality and insults, but we were loyal to each other, and best friends. I sat in his worn-out caster chair and skimmed over the mass of papers strewn over his desk.

The moment I saw the words, *Autopsy Report,* I knew I was on the right playing field.

Little in my life ever goes the way I would like it. If being unlucky, unfortunate, and unappreciated were a social cause, I would be the poster boy. However, God must have been looking the other way that day and took a breather on making my life miserable. Grossy's phone rattled, and when he picked it up, the screaming withered his ear. *"Detective Grosslein, get your ass in here, now. This is a meeting and you are not going to miss it. Do you understand?"*

His face dropped to his knees and he turned a sickly gray. "Yes, sir. Right there." Stomping out the door, I heard him mumble, "Fucking meeting. I forgot." He turned and pointed his finger at me, snarling, "Get out of here."

"Thank you, God." A moment later I had made copies of the coroner's report on Elwood Pierpont, and, miracle of miracles, it also included the report on the bloody victim in the front seat. I then hurried out to the street before Grossy realized he had left for his meeting without the report. As I hustled down the street, it occurred to me that for my good fortune, God was going to really crap on me as a payback.

Sitting in my car I poured over the details. Pierpont had been strangled with a leather thong resulting in asphyxiation. There was severe bruising on his back, about the size of a softball, and the thong was applied from the back. There were also bruises on his wrists and shoulders, in the front. It wasn't mentioned in the report, but I got a pretty good picture of what went down. The most interesting item was the trace of vaginal fluid on his penis and lips.

The next page showed the confusing colored diagram of DNA from the fluid trace. It was identified as belonging to Laura Blake. The rap sheet on Laura Blake had her arrested more times for prostitution than I had in visiting girls just like her. The mug shot showed a gorgeous face with long wavy dark hair. Damn, another Cheryl look-alike. The rap on the guy who messed up the front of the Caddy had him as Larry Carter, with no known connection to anything. He was logged as the killer mainly due to his presence and the knee-sized bruise on Elwood's back, sort of fitting in size. I had trouble with that concept, thinking that with a guy of his size, if he knelt on Elwood to strangle him, he'd break his back. Another loose end.

It wasn't in the report, but I knew the cops were as interested in the hooker as I was. To them, she was under suspicion for a double homicide. To me, she most likely was walking around with a fortune in bearer bonds. I knew that at some point I was going to have to get Grossy drunk and wheedle the name of the Caddy owner out of him.

Feeling a flair of bravado, I entered HellBurgers through the front door, just like a real customer. As usual, the place was packed, but I spotted a vacancy at the end of the bar. Settling onto the stool, I remembered the lovely and horney Kathleen calling me a bourbon man, so I reinforced the vision and ordered a double, neat. I was salivating over the bowl of pretzels, three stools down, but I was hesitant to possibly lose my seat to anyone by getting up to fetch them. Prodding the woman next to me, I used my suave and debonair voice to ask, "Hey, can you reach the pretzels for me?"

The Hulk Hogan look-alike turned to me and said, "Fuck you. Get 'em yourself."

A pro at being rebuffed, I was not deterred. I countered with, "I'll share them with you." I added a smile to sweeten the deal.

This woman looked like she could spit nails through concrete. I'd rather kiss Dog the Bounty Hunter than cross horns with her, but she told me, "Buy me and my old man a drink, and I'll think about it."

Shit, man, for a bowl of free pretzels? I gave in, "Yeah sure, tell the bar boy what you want." They were served a couple of highballs. The two accepted the drinks, got up and left. The bowl of pretzels still sat three stools away.

"Ten bucks, Norby."

I passed him a ten and asked, "Hey, Pappy, can you slide the pretzels down here? Please?"

He obliged me and asked, "Mitch know you're here?"

"No, but I want to talk to him."

Pappy picked up the phone, mumbled something into it, looked back at me and sneered. He was nice enough to come back and tell me, "He says if you ain't gone in ten minutes, he's gonna throw you out."

Ah, at last a connection. I waited another hour and downed three more bourbon doubles. If Mitch didn't show up soon I was going to hit the floor.

I was certain Mitch let me sit here for an hour because my money was going into his till. He had thrown out drunks before, and he never hesitated to throw me out. However, much to his annoyance, I kept coming back. Mitch finally showed up and sat down next to me. By his expression I couldn't tell if he was planning to beat the crap out of me or have a civil conversation. Fortune was on my side. He asked, "What gives, Norby? Pappy said you needed to talk."

My mind was sliding away from the bourbon, and the pretzels were making me sick. "Hi, Mitch, nice of you to drop in."

"As long as you were buying drinks, I wasn't going to interrupt the flow. I asked what you wanted."

I pulled out the mug shot of Laura Blake and held it in front of him. "You ever seen her around?"

His gaze lingered long enough to tell me he did indeed know the woman. "Why you want her?"

"Doesn't matter, Mitch. I need to talk to her."

"You can't afford her, Klein. Find a nice trollop to satisfy your lust."

"Trollops won't work, Mitch. I need this one."

He looked at the picture a long moment, seemingly to recall old family memories from an album. "She in trouble?"

"Yeah, she's in trouble, Mitch. Where is she?"

"You'd be better off with the trollop, buddy. This one's trouble and the crowd she works for is worse than trouble. Look for a pimp by the name of Billy Cummings. Tall, thin wiry dude with greasy black hair."

Excited at getting a connection, I asked, "They work out of here?"

He handed the picture back and said, "Not no more. I had to hire a couple of goons to convince him to take his stable elsewhere. He went over to the Conestoga, but since they moved up from the lakeshore, their act's cleaner and they don't have no room for the likes of him. He's working the call-in trade now. I heard he's got some high rollers on the list that pay primo for good head and stuff."

Bingo, getting closer. "Like Ambassador Pierpont?"

Mitch looked at me closely, clearly wondering just how intimate he should get with his knowledge. "He's dead, ain't he?"

"Yup, as a door nail. This babe had a trace of her special juice on him."

Mitch stood up and told me, "I heard something like that. Be careful, Norbs, this ain't no high school dating club."

Sliding off the stool, I tried to be cordial, offering, "See ya, Mitch. Thanks for the booze."

He, being cordial as well, "Thanks for buying it."

Back in my Reliant, I called Jeanine. "Hi, honey. I want you to check on someone for me. Two people, in fact." If there was any information on Laura Blake or Billy Cummings, my girl would grab it.

The Reliant managed to start, so I went home to talk to Hanky some more. With a description of this Cummings dude, maybe my derelict friend could ID him.

CHAPTER EIGHT

• • • • • • • • • • • • • • • • • • • •

Black Bear Hotel.

NERVOUS ABOUT HANGING AROUND TOO LONG, Laura tried subtly to move Donald Portman into getting back on the road. Giving in to his plea for a quickie, she used a few moves to facilitate his pleasure. Rolling off, he moaned, "Oh, Laura, where did you learn to do that?"

Jumping off the bed, she reached for his hand, pulling at him. "Come on, horney. Get me to Minneapolis and I'll show you some more."

With nothing to pack, they were ready in minutes. Timed as a last minute request just as they were at the door to leave, "Oh, Don, could I call my sister? I want to tell her I'll be going to the Cities."

Handing her his cell phone, she punched in the numbers, then said, "Carrie? Hi, it's me. Just a minute." Doing a good pee-pee dance, she mouthed the words to Don, "I gotta go. Be right out." Her voice back into the phone, she went on, "Yeah, hang on, Carrie. I gotta hit the john." Behind the closed bathroom door, she frantically whispered, "Carrie, can you talk?"

"Yeah, Laura, where are you? What's going on?"

"Carrie, listen, I picked up a guy and we're at the Black Bear on I-35. He's taking me to Minneapolis. I'm going to see if he'll put me up. Get away from Billy as fast as you can. I'll call you tomorrow so we can get away. Get to Minneapolis and keep your phone on."

Carrie, excitedly asked, "Laura, where in Minneapolis? Billy's hopping mad. What did you do?"

"We'll talk when we get together. We'll have all the money we need to break away, Carrie. Gotta go."

• •

Carrie closed her cell phone and handed it to Billy. “She’s at the Black Bear. Some dude picked her up and is taking her to the Cities. That’s all she told me.” She looked intently at Billy, waiting to see if he was going to explode.

Instead, he grinned, and said, “Come on. We’re going to find them.”

Familiar with a few of the desk clerks at the Black Bear, Billy hoped one of them was on duty. Having set up meetings with his girls and a few well-healed gamblers, it was a good gig. Moving from the tables in the casino to the bed in the hotel was a natural.

Billy strode up to the Black Bear Hotel reception desk with his story all planned. The clerk approached him, “Sir, may I help you?”

This was not one of his contacts, but he didn’t have time to wait. With the best distraught look he could muster, Billy said, “My wife. My wife was here.” He put a tremor to his lips and squeezed a drop of moisture from one eye.

Confused, the clerk asked, “Sir? I don’t understand.” He tilted his head and leaned forward.

Billy slid a picture of Laura across the counter. “My wife was here with another guy. She left me, and I know this guy is going to hurt her. Please.”

“Sir, even if I did know, I just couldn’t tell you. Policy, you know.”

Billy laid a twenty on top of the picture. “She’s in danger. I’ve got to get to her.”

“Have you called the police?”

Getting frustrated, Billy got louder, “Yes, I did. Of course, I did, but they aren’t doing anything.” One more twenty was set on top of the first one. “What’s it going to take for you to do the right thing and save her life? Please.”

A third twenty joined the others. The clerk picked up the picture, along with the money, and pondered a moment. “Well, come to think of it, if it’s important, I saw a woman who looked just like this walk across the parking lot and get into a maroon Mercury. About two hours ago.”

Billy clenched the counter edge, wailing, “Yes, that’s his car. Oh, God, he’s going to hurt her. I just know it. He’s up to no good. Please, give me his address.”

Backing up, the clerk held his hands out, “Oh, no, I can’t do that. Uh, uh.” His hands slowly lowered and his eyes grew to the size of saucers as Billy thumbed a wad of hundred-dollar bills at him.

Five minutes later, Billy was back in the car, holding up a piece of paper with the name of Donald Portman, and his address. Smiling, he leaned over to give Carrie a soft kiss. "See, honey? People will sell out their mother if the price is right."

• •

Back at the Duluth police station, on First Street, Detective Stuart Grosslein received a note. The dispatcher who handed it to him explained, "A clerk at the Black Bear called and said he was concerned about some woman who might be in trouble."

Holding the note, Grosslein mumbled, "What the hell am I going to do about this? The county sheriff should get this. Did the clerk give you any details?"

"A little. He said some guy was in looking for her, said she took off with some other guy who was going to hurt her."

"Yeah, all right. I'll give them a call."

The dispatcher turned to leave, but stopped, "Oh, Detective Grosslein, Norbert Klein's waiting to see you."

"Oh, shit. I don't have time for him. Tell him that . . ." Abruptly, Detective Grosslein stopped. He picked up the note he had been handed and said, "Never mind. Send him in. Thanks."

Ten seconds later, Norbert Klein strode in, "Morning, Grossy. I got a question for you. Where'd the Caddy Pierpont was in come from?"

Not looking up, Grosslein answered, "What brings you in so early?"

"I woke up alone and got lonesome for company. Since I love you so much, I just needed to be close to you. What about the Caddy? Who's it registered to?"

"It was reported stolen, Klein. That's all you get."

"Yeah, it was hot. I figured that. But at some point, there has to be a name on that thirty-thousand-dollar car. Or, was it yours?"

"Funny, smart ass." Grosslein pushed back, asking, "Say, since you're in here all the time, how would you like to become a pretend cop and do some leg work and not get paid for it?"

Norbert grinned. "Gee, how can I turn that down? Why? You wouldn't ask me for anything unless you were desperate."

"What I'm desperate for is to get you out of my hair."

"Grossy, you gotta stop banging your head against the headboard. Your running out of hair."

"Fuck you, Klein. You want to do this or not?"

• •

An hour later, Norbert Klein, now an unpaid official Duluth Police Scout, stood at the counter in the lobby of the Black Bear Hotel. Getting a semblance of a story from the nervous clerk, Norby had a hunch. Holding the mug shot of Laura Blake in front of him, he could tell right away he had struck the motherlode.

"Yeah, that's her. I only got a glimpse as she walked through the parking lot, but she's quite attractive and . . . well, she looked nice."

"The guy who was asking . . . describe him."

"Hmm, sort of a mobster type, actually. Cheap looking, tall, thin, dark hair."

Smiling, Klein asked, "You mean like a pimp would look?"

"I guess so."

Leaning closer, Norbert asked, in a low voice, "Now, what else can you tell me that you know you shouldn't? Did you give this mobster-type guy any information that might lead to where the idiot with the babe was going?"

"I can't tell you any more. Sorry, I'm done here. I just thought at the time that the woman might be in trouble. That's all."

"Well, turns out you're right. The woman is in trouble, but it's from the snarky guy you gave the address to who's going to kill her. Now, give me the same info, or I'll have you in a holding cell waiting to see a judge on charges of impeding an investigation."

Horrified, the clerk copied Donald's name and address. Handing it over, he said, "She'll be all right, won't she?"

"She's a hooker and greasy guy's her pimp. If anyone gets racked, it'll be the poor dope who's with her. Have a nice day."

Chapter Nine

Stopping at a Travelodge in the South Minneapolis suburb of Bloomington, Donald Portman used his credit card to guarantee a two-week stay.

"Don, won't your wife question the charges on the card?" Laura asked.

"I don't care, Laura. I don't want to let you go. You can stay here until I can find an apartment or something. I'm not just going to dump you and forget about you. I want to take care of you. I chose this place because it's not too far from where I live. I can come and see you more often."

"That's sweet of you, Don. I'll always be here for you, whenever you can get away. I promise, I will repay you as soon as I can, honey. Do you have time for a quickie before you go home?"

Laura stepped into the personal-gratification role and became a prostitute again. After making him giddy with happiness and sexual satisfaction, she finagled two-hundred dollars from him. After he left, she walked to Wal-Mart for a few items of clothing, then started trolling for sex-starved men waiting to be satisfied. At the end of two days, she had accumulated almost two thousand dollars, and upgraded her wardrobe. Her new earnings and a friendship with Omar, the night shift Travelodge clerk, gained her a phony Texas driver's license and sufficient identification to pass off her new image. Mobility became the only remaining tool she needed. Borrowing Omar's car, she was ready to become a business tycoon.

Dressed in a dark power suit, a Gucci bag under her arm and high heels that were designed to make noise on a marble floor, Laura entered the lobby of the Fidelity Trust Bank, on Eighth Street and Marquette Avenue. Sunglasses gave a mysterious illusion she used as part of her guise. Doing her homework ahead of her entry, Laura clacked her way to the information desk, announcing, "I'd like to see Henry Fairchild, please."

The young receptionist looked up and did a double take at the beautiful woman standing before her desk. Lightly asking, "Do you have an appointment?"

Laura feigned an indignant air, lowering her sunglasses enough to view the girl at the desk. Handing her business card to her, Laura said, "My dear girl, I don't *need* an appointment. Point me to his office before I buy this mausoleum and throw your skinny ass to the wolves. Now, give him a call, and tell him I'm on the way."

Rapidly responding, the woman's finger punched the right button, telling the opposite end of the connection, "Mrs. Pamela Vanderguild is here to see Mr. Fairchild." Responding to the inquiry, the girl said, "No, she doesn't. She's the CEO of Vanderguild Oil, in Dallas." Lowering her voice and cupping the receiver, she whispered, "Please, Debby, work her in. She's not in a good mood. Okay, thanks." Turning her smile to Mrs. Vanderguild, the girl said, "Mr. Fairchild will see you. The guard will escort you."

Pushing the sunglasses back to the bridge of her nose, Mrs. Vanderguild said, "Of course he will."

In the plushly appointed secretarial chamber, the haughty woman behind the walnut desk asked, "And what is it you need to see Mr. Fairchild about?"

"Would the number ten-million get you off your fat ass and announce me? Or should I just walk in and complain about you?"

Startled, the secretary stood and nervously said, "Of course, this way please."

Mr. Henry Fairchild stood and extended his hand to the tall attractive woman. "Mrs. Vanderguild. Please, have a seat. Would you like some coffee?"

Seating herself to expose a shapely bare leg to Mr. Fairchild, Laura said, "No thank you."

Sitting back in his leather chair, Mr. Fairchild positioned himself to be able to ogle the leg. "Your entrance has raised some consternation with my staff. I'm not familiar with you, but your insistence got you in. How may I help you?"

The bank president's attention was not so much waiting for an answer as it was wanting to stroke that leg. The stark whiteness of his thinning hair said all that needed to be said for his age and his health.

Reaching out to pass the phony business card to him, she said, "I want to deposit ten-million dollars in this bank. Can you guarantee the safety of my money?"

"Of course, Fidelity Trust is one of..."

Interrupting, she said, "I know all about your bank. That's why I chose it. I want to open an account to finance a chain of gas stations and possibly a refinery. I have plans to acquire Super America, possibly Holiday. Maybe both. We'll see. I might make a stab at the Koch refinery. Anyway, I want to cash some bearer bonds, do more research on my acquisitions, and then deposit the ten-million." She reached into the Gucci bag and pulled out two one-hundred-thousand-dollar bonds. She adjusted her voice to be snappy, direct, and to the point. A definite "no nonsense" attitude indicated that there would be no questions asked. "Cash these, deposit ten-thousand, and I'll take the rest in currency. I also want two safety deposit boxes, not located together."

Happily accepting the bonds, Henry said, "Of course. I'll have Virginia take care of it immediately." Returning from the secretary's chamber, he asked, "Are you sure you wouldn't like something to drink?" Opening a wall panel, he exposed a mirror that reflected on a very sophisticated arrangement of liquor.

Standing, she strode to him putting her hand gently on his shoulder. "A Drambuie would be nice. Neat if you don't mind."

For the next twenty minutes Laura entertained the gray-haired man. She had the idea that if she could get him into bed, her whole game plan could take a quick and satisfying turn. On the verge of asking him to have dinner with her, she was interrupted by Virginia entering with her cash, a deposit slip, and the safety deposit keys.

Standing, Laura took Mr. Fairchild's hand, telling him, "Well, it's been a pleasure meeting you, Henry. I'd love to have dinner with you some evening. I'll give you a call."

Hoisting the Gucci to her shoulder, Mrs. Pamela Vanderguild left the happy office to complete her business. Her first stop was at the safety deposit department. The teller had used the bank's duplicate key to open the boxes, then left Mrs. Vanderguild alone. Quickly dismantling Elwood's brief case, she divided the bonds putting half into each drawer. "If one is found, the other one may be missed." Pleased at her logic, she assembled herself and strode confidently out the front door. She tossed the empty valise into a trash can.

Her first responsibility would be to pay off Donald Portman and encourage him to mend his marriage. Once he was out of her hair, she could start building her new life. She thought of a new name, new place . . . hell, why not a new country, even plastic surgery to hide herself completely. It was almost time to get hold of Carrie. Then they would both be free.

At the same time that Laura was becoming a wealthy businesswoman, the Portman home was getting visitors. Answering the ring of the doorbell, Mrs. Portman asked, "Yes, may I help you?" The nice-looking man standing before her, and the blonde woman with him, presented her with something she couldn't turn down.

Billy's silver tongue slid his message out, "Mrs. Portman, my associate and I are starting a neighborhood bible study group. Would you be interested?"

Thrilled to be asked to help spread the word of the Lord, Melanie Portman let the man and woman into her house. Clearing some toys off the sofa, Mrs. Portman said, "Please make yourselves at home. I'll get some refreshments. Then you can tell me about your plan." Never one to turn her back on the word of the Lord, she offered them coffee and cookies before they saved her soul. Billy followed her around the small kitchen, helping to make coffee and offering advice on household hints. Carrie sat on the sofa in a staring contest with a talkative three-year-old boy, who asked, "Whadda you want? I'm Bobby. Who are you? Wanna play?"

Smiling, she nervously told him, "We're gonna talk about Jesus."

The front door burst open. A pretty young girl called out, "Mom, I brought Mickey home from next door." When she saw Carrie, she stumbled and stared at her. Nodding to the stranger, the girl took four-year-old Mickey into the kitchen.

Carrie sat, bewildered, wondering just what the hell Billy was going to do with this bunch. It was becoming comical. She could hear introductions in the kitchen.

Mrs. Portman came from the kitchen with a tray of cookies. Billy followed with a pot of coffee and a pitcher of Kool Aid in the other hand. Standing up with a smile, he placed his hand on the girl's shoulder, asking, "Stephanie, would you please bring in enough kitchen chairs so we may all sit in a circle?"

Next, he passed his infectious smile to Mrs. Portman, "Melanie, this may sound strange, but do you happen to have any duct tape?"

Startled, but anxious to help, she quickly answered, "Of course."

With the Portman family sitting in the kitchen chairs, Melanie asked, "Now, what is it you wanted?" Her smile beamed through the room until it caught the slightly altered expression on Billy's face. The idea that something was wrong crossed her mind for the first time.

Even after Billy had them all trussed tightly to the chairs with duct tape, she asked, "Are we going to talk about Jesus now?" Her tone begged for explanation and was edged with dwindling hope.

The next step was to cover all their mouths with more duct tape. Then Billy explained, "No, Mrs. Portman. We're not much interested in Jesus, come to think of it. We're going to sit here quietly and wait for your husband to come home to join our discussion group."

He stood back to admire his work, awed by just how trusting and stupid these people were. Carrie pressed to his side, quietly asking, "Billy, what's going to happen here?"

Not looking at her he said, "You're not as dumb as them, are you? Figure it out, honey. We're here to get answers, and this is a guaranteed way to do it." He leered at her with a vicious sneer. "Just don't get in the way. When I need you, be ready. Go close the blinds on all these windows."

Carrie backed up, not liking what was going on. Being controlled by Billy as much as the Portmans were, she knew enough to keep her mouth shut.

Donald arrived home a little later that evening, dragging his tired body through the door. If Laura had been at the Travelodge, instead of picking up a john at Joe Sensor's Sports Bar, he wouldn't have come home at all, which would have been a very good thing for him. As he stepped into his living room, his first thought was that his family was playing a game. "No, I'm too tired for games. Melanie, just what nonsense are you . . ."

He stopped, dumbly staring at his wife, his twelve-year-old daughter, and the four-year-old and three-year-old sons, tied to kitchen chairs in the middle of his living room. A fifth chair sat empty next to his wife. Understanding took a moment to travel to his brain, but when he recognized the duct tape stretched across their mouths, the alarm sounded loudly. Rushing through the room, he tripped on Billy's foot, landing on top of his whimpering wife, topling her over. Unable to struggle against Billy's powerful strangle hold, Don was forced into the other kitchen chair while a blonde woman tied him securely to it, duct tape screeching as it was unrolled.

His wife lay helplessly on her side straining to look at her husband. The duct tape was restricting her breathing, and panic was quickly setting in.

Screaming through his fear and confusion, Donald demanded, "What is this? What do you want? We don't have any money." Leaning forward on his chair, he strained against his bonds.

Billy backhanded his face. "We don't want your money, Mr. Portman. All we want is her." Billy held a photograph of Laura's smiling face in front of him.

Don's stomach erupted, emptying down his front. "Oh, God, no. Laura." He looked at the angry stranger, pathetically asking, "What is this? What do you want with us?" The sour stench of Don's lunch hung on his chin, soaking his shirtfront. His tears came slowly as he hung his head, "Oh, no."

Collecting his nerves, Don looked up defiantly, challenging his captor. "So you found her, you worm. Do you get off beating your wife? You don't deserve her, and she's going to divorce you. She's got proof, you know."

Donald's confused wife looked up fiercely at him. Screaming through the duct tape, her words were muffled, *"Who is Laura? why are we tied up and gagged?"*

Amused, Billy crouched in front of Donald. "Is that what she told you, you sap? That I was her husband?" His head flew back, bellowing out laughter. Rapidly switching to a severe voice, "You stupid shit. She's not my wife. She's a hooker, you moron. She's a fucking whore, and she's been fucking you."

Afraid of looking at his wife, Donald knew he was going to have to tell her everything when this was over. He also knew he might be the one getting served divorse papers. Melanie glared at him, screaming through the duct tape.

Billy hit Donald again. "Where is she? Tell me where she is and you and your drab little family can go back to your drab little life here. You said she had proof of something. What? What did she have?"

Numb, Don whispered, "In the case. She had a case of proof that you beat her. You shouldn't hit a woman. She's going to get you good."

The case. Excited, Billy asked, "What did the case look like? Was it black leather, about this big?" His hands estimated the size of Elwood's case.

Looking and feeling extremely dumb, Don answered, "Yes, that's what she had."

Making sure that Donald took him seriously, Billy grabbed him by the hair, yanking him backwards and screaming, "*Where is she?*"

Way out of his league, trembling, Don spilled everything he knew, "I got her a room at the Bloomington Travelodge. Room 17. Please leave us alone now."

"Did she have the case with her?"

"Yes, she did. Go away now, please." Donald's head hung in submissive shame as his family, tied up around him, stared at him.

Billy had driven all the way to Minneapolis and he wasn't going to leave until he took care of business, and more importantly, covered his tracks. "You're a family man, Donald. You have no business spending money on whores."

Melanie was reeling from what she was hearing, but her disgust for her husband sent her into panic. The revulsion and horror forced her stomach to push its bile up into her mouth, the vomit spewing out the edges of the duct tape. Melanie Portman gagged, drowning in her own disgorge. Convulsing, in her chair, her body twitched, and she struggled against her bonds and the choking vomit. As her efforts weakened, she rolled her head over to stare at her husband, her eyes open but no longer seeing.

Donald, his mouth hanging open, stared at her, dumb and unbelieving.

Billy took the 9-mm pistol from the holster under his arm and slowly screwed the silencer to it. Walking over to three-year-old Bobby, he put the muzzle to the child's head and pulled the trigger. The noise from the grown-ups arguing in the room was the only thing the child feared, not understanding that guns killed people. The back of his small head exploded, his large blue eyes staring wide open at the ceiling, slumping in his chair. The red dot on his forehead started weeping down his face.

Don and twelve year old Stephanie were madly jumping in their chairs trying to inch their way to the destruction taking place. Screaming through her tape, Stephanie fell over and writhed wildly on the floor, while Donald watched helplessly as four year old Michael was next to have his brains blown out the back of his head.

Carrie screamed, "For God's sake, you ass hole, stop. *Stop.*" Rushing to Billy to put an end to the madness, she was stopped by the next bullet as it tore through her shoulder, sending her to the floor.

The carnage resumed. Donald had maneuvered his chair close to his daughter and he tried to protect her by leaning over the paralyzed Stephanie. It was a futile effort. Billy pressed the muzzle to her forehead, but her body had already shut down, going limp. Her eyes rolled back into her head. Billy had frightened the girl to death, yet he squeezed the trigger anyway.

Donald's screaming had ruptured his larynx, and he had gone silent. Blood oozed from his contorted mouth. Helplessly struggling toward Billy, dragging the chair with him, he bumped into Billy's leg, pushing as hard as he could. He fell sideways under the legs of the chair, his useless, scraping words going nowhere. "*No, no, no, oh, my God, no.*" The terror ended for Donald Portman as the gun was put to his temple. *Phhht, phhht* as the silencer spit death from the muzzle. He used two bullets to kill Dad, just because he wasn't done playing yet. Scanning the carnage, Billy smiled at the mess he made, thinking that now, he could hardly wait to get to Laura.

Putting a fresh clip into the pistol, Billy turned to make certain that Carrie was dead also. To his surprise, she no longer lay where the shoulder shot had dropped her. He ran for the door. The Buick was gone also.

• •

Carrie pushed the Buick to its limit getting away from the Portman house. Screeching into a gas station, she frantically yelled at the startled clerk, "Where's the Bloomington Travelodge. Please, I gotta know now." Her right arm hung loose, and blood had spread over her shoulder.

Following a hastily sketched map by the clerk, Carrie landed the Buick at the Travelodge. Pounding on the door to Room 17, Carrie yelled, "Laura, open. Hurry." The door flew open pulling Carrie in with the force.

Laura gasped. "Oh, my God. Get in here, quick."

Blood covered the front of Carrie, and was spreading across her back. Carefully stripping the shirt off, Laura washed her, and then held clean towels to the entrance and exit wounds. "It went through. If it didn't cut anything too badly inside, you're going to be all right. We need to get some bandages and disinfectant."

Frantic, Carrie yelled, "We don't have time for anything. We have to get out of here before Billy shows up."

Thrown into a new level of fear, Laura babbled, "Billy? He knows where we are?"

Frantically yelling, "No shit, woman. I found you. He's got to be right behind me."

"Okay, okay, let's just think. What in hell are we going to do?"

Carrie got off the bed, staggering to the door, shouting, "Fuck the think part, we have to get out of here. Don't you understand anything?"

With Laura's coat draped over Carrie's bloody body, they drove the Buick to a different neighborhood. Stopping in a parking lot, Laura shut the engine off, trying to think. "All right, Carrie, how did you find me?"

Worn out, she sullenly answered, "That Donald guy told Billy."

"*Don*? How did you find *him*?" Then, knowing Billy, she demanded, "What happened to him? Is he okay? What did Billy do?"

Carrie's head fell back onto the headrest, tears flowing down her cheeks and sobs wreaking her body.

"They're all dead. Billy killed them all. The mom, all three kids, and the dad. He shot them all just to play with them. Just fucking shot them dead. I tried to stop him, and he did this to me. We're just fucking pieces of meat to him, Laura." She squeezed her eyes shut, "When he was shooting the girl, I crawled outside."

Carrie's face puckered in fear, rolling against the headrest. She wailed, "The kids, oh, God, not the kids. The kids, Laura. Little boys. Just toddlers. The mom and the kids, just wasted like nothing."

Horrified, Laura demanded, "You left before Don was shot? How do you know he was killed?"

Rolling her head to face Laura, Carrie slowly said, "Why wouldn't he kill him?"

Squeezing her face with her fists, Laura choked out, "I did that to them, Carrie. I was the reason they all died." With solemn resolve, Laura said, "My life isn't worth a shit to anybody, but I promise that before I die, I'll make that bastard pay."

Dejected and all but giving up, Carrie moaned, "Who gives a shit? We're all gonna die."

Agitated, Laura firmly said, "No, we're not, babe. We're going to start thinking smarter and get out of this. First, we have to dump this car and get a place to stay. Then we'll get you taken care of."

Paying five-thousand dollars cash, Laura bought a used Toyota, leaving Billy's Buick abandoned in the street. They rented a small apartment near the Uptown area of Minneapolis, trying to blend with the artsy-fartsy society of hippie wanna-be's, artists, and closer to women who earned their living on their backs, like they did.

The bullet had passed through the fleshy part of Carrie's shoulder, so if an internal infection didn't set in, she could live on Tylenol and sport a large gauze bandage on both sides of her shoulder. For the next week, the two kept to themselves with a great deal of concern over a red patch that had surrounded the wound. Taking a chance, Laura asked the building caretaker if she knew of a doctor who would keep his mouth shut in exchange for a bonus.

The large Latino woman told her, "For a hundred bucks my mouth will work."

Understanding that bribery by desperate people was just a means of survival, Laura dug into her stash of money. Handing over five twenties, Laura asked, "How do I know I can trust him?"

Smiling, the large woman said, "You just trusted *me*, didn't you? Come inside."

Stepping into her apartment that stank of garlic, chiriso, and cigarette smoke, she turned to Laura, "It's me, honey. I'm your doctor. I lost my license ten years ago, but I still manage to fix a few people. Bring your friend and five-hundred dollars tonight. I'll give her an antibiotic and check her over."

After a disinfectant swab and a few stitches, a disgruntled Carrie said, "Is she the only quack around? I wouldn't let her fix my horse."

"Carrie, she did what needed to be done. Besides, you don't have a horse."

A couple weeks later, the tedium of lying low and doing nothing came to a head. They had almost one-hundred-eighty thousand dollars in cash stashed in the apartment. Carrie kept pressing Laura to turn in the rest of the bonds. "For God's sake, woman, get the cash and let's split. We can't stay holed up here any longer before we kill each other."

"Carrie, I'm as anxious as you are to get the money, but I'm also anxious to live a little longer. As long as Billy is alive, we're in trouble. Then, all we have to worry about is the goddamn syndicate. You and I both know Billy's a cupcake next to those guys."

Frustrated and bored, Carrie said, "But we sit here forever doing nothing?"

"No. Okay, listen. We'll cash two more bonds each, split it and both go our separate ways. That's almost a quarter of a million apiece, babe. It'll get us out of here."

Relaxing at the prospect, Carrie asked the obvious, "When?"

"That's a good question. I don't know." Laura's answer was solemn. She favored staying out of sight for as long as possible.

Carrie had more temper than brains and didn't use either one very well. She was the one person who would have succeeded under Billy's control because he did all the thinking for her. He considered her stupid, yet controllable. Her brilliant blonde hair was a sharp contrast to Laura's dark mane, giving his clients a choice. His plans had been to branch into the lucrative field of pornography, specializing in lesbian movies with his two favorite girls. His bosses agreed that the contrast between them would be stunning.

In the meantime, Carrie decided to get back in the game. Her wound was healing, but was a distraction. She'd cut her fee. The next Saturday night, Laura was getting agitated at Carrie's being gone so long, until at about one in the morning the phone rang.

"Laura, it's me. I got arrested for prostitution."

CHAPTER TEN

Laura and Carrie's apartment, the Uptown area, South Minneapolis.

LAURA YELLED INTO THE PHONE, "You got what?"

I'm sorry. I was out pushing some trade, and I got busted. They want some bail money. Can you come and get me out?"

Laura had little choice but to ablige. Riding back to the apartment, Laura was fuming, "What were you thinking? We've got enough money stashed away to take care of anything we need. Don't you realize that Billy might still be wandering around this city looking for us?"

Hiding behind her hand, Carrie weakly said, "Don't lecture me, you're not my mother."

Showing more compassion, Laura told her, "We'll cash in those bonds and get out of here as soon as possible."

With a sarcastic response, Carrie chided, "Gee, where have I heard that before?"

"Yeah, I know. I was being way too cautious. Now we gotta get out." Looking over at Carrie, Laura could sense she had something to say but was holding back. "What's on your mind? Spit it out."

"The cop!"

"What cop?"

"The one that busted me. She was undercover."

"So?"

Sighing, Carrie said, "She said something about her following up on what I was doing to get out of the trade. She wants to come and see us."

"That's some new shit. Well, maybe we'll be gone before she gets to it." After a pause, Laura added, "Why can't they just arrest us and let us go? They think they're going to save us from a horrible life. No shit."

Looking at her partner, Carrie said, "Laura, look at us. This *is* a horrible life. I'd really like to go home without thinking I had to be a whore to make a pimp rich. We're slaves, Laura, just goddamn slaves. All I want is to go home without getting shit on and people treating me like dirt. I don't want to be embarrassed to walk on the same street with normal people."

• •

The Uptown District, Minneapolis.

Detective Yolanda Brown checked the address on Humboldt Avenue South, murmuring to herself, "You dumb shit, you gave me your correct address? You should never give a cop the right house number." Working her way to the second floor, she followed the odors and filth of more than half a century of people's lives. The yellowed walls were permeated with ethnic cooking fallout from whatever population was in force at the time. Jewish, Polish, German, Hmong—it didn't matter. They were the immigrants of society trying to survive from one day to the next. Their sons died on the street, and the daughters laid on their backs looking for the promised good life. Escaping the tyranny of politics, armies, and war, they were surrounded by a different kind of war. This one had no victor and no happy ending. This was the war of poverty and ignorance.

Stopping in front of number twelve, she gently knocked, hoping there was nobody home so she could just leave. The door pulled partially open with a beautiful dark-haired woman filling in the opening. "Yes?" Her voice was calm, but held a defiant edge to it.

"I came to see Carrie Wallace. Is she home?"

The woman looked at Yolanda for a moment before asking, "Why?"

The response, while impertinent, was the obvious one. Handing her a business card, the detective said said, "Yolanda Brown. Call me Yo-yo. I'm the one who arrested her. I said I'd be by to talk to her. If she's home. Do you mind if I come in?" The undercover policewoman would rather be in the middle of a street fight than standing in the smelly hallway. Her nervous system was starting to retaliate, screaming for a can of Mountain Dew, or mainline caffeine.

Yolanda never looked like she was standing still. Her motors were constantly running wide open, giving her the look of a racehorse held back at the gate. The springy black curls covering her head bounced as her body shook and bopped to an imaginary rap tune. She tried to camouflage the sparse spot on the back of her head, but no matter what she did, the memory of how it got there could never be hidden . . . or forgotten.

Backing away, the woman in the doorway said, "Sure, I guess so."

Carrie was taken back by the slim black woman standing in their living room. "Officer Brown. I didn't think you'd actually come and visit."

Twitching in front of the two women, Yolanda truthfully admitted, "I didn't either. I'm doing this on my own, and I don't really know how this is going to play out."

The dark depressing living room sported maybe three pieces of worn-out furniture. Dark oak woodwork lent a gloomy feeling, emphasized by the threadbare carpet. The only light source other than the filthy windows came from a dim overhead bulb hanging on a cloth-covered cord. The collection of foul odors in the hallway had settled in here also.

With everyone seated, Laura asked, "Do all the hookers you book get the personal attention of the arresting officer? Wouldn't it be easier to just fine them and let them go?"

"Yeah, I suppose it would, but where would that get us?" Yolanda offered a sad smile, but got nothing in return.

Carrie was getting agitated. "What do you know about it anyway? You're just a cop. You don't have to put up with the down-in-the-dirt shit. At night you get to go home and live like a human." Carrie's temper waned. She waved as if to cancell her anger and said, "People like us just get shit on. You remember what slavery is don't you? Well, we're in it and there isn't going to be a fucking civil war to end it."

Understanding her frustration, Yolanda quietly answered, "I *do* know what it's about. Yeah, I know about the shit you gotta take, and the beatings from the pimps, and the abuse from slimy goons sticking their dick into any opening they can find. You see me as a cop, but I've done my time on my back, and my knees. I work vice undercover, but on my own I fuck. I do solos in my spare time. That ain't right either, but I manage to get a boatload of perverts off the street doing it. That's the difference between you and me. I got a badge and the legal right to bust mother fuckers I don't like. I get paid for doing it. And, I don't have no asshole whipping me and taking everything I earn."

Yolanda sat forward, knowing she had made a mistake coming here. "What I *do* have that no man is going to take from me is my self-respect. Lose that, honey, and you lose it all. I saw you working the johns, and man, you're good, girl, but not good enough to stay away from me. The trouble with you doing tricks is that the goon just goes back on the street, and spreads what ever bug either one of you is carrying at the time. He finds out that picking up a babe on the street works, and then moves his game up to younger meat, school kids. The next step is rape, and we don't like that at all."

Standing up, Yolanda said, "I'm sorry for coming in here like this. I just thought that if I could get you to think about flipping hamburgers instead of your ass, I'd be doing something good in a fucked up world."

As she paused at the door, the dark-haired woman said, "Thanks. We appreciate your concern. Who knows... we'll probably never do tricks again."

Detective Brown shrugged and snickered, "Yeah, and pigs don't stink."

Yolanda handed Laura her business card, saying, "Give me a call if you need help." Then, as an afterthought, she looked at Carrie, "I destroyed your arrest record. Stay off the street and you'll be clean." Bopping her way out to her car, she had a gentle feeling that maybe she did something good coming here. "I hope it lasts for them."

Behind the closed door, Carrie looked at Laura with an astonished stare, whispering, "Oh, my God, do you believe that?"

CHAPTER ELEVEN

I GREW UP IN SOUTH MINNEAPOLIS LOOKING FOR, and usually finding, trouble with my chum, Stu Grosslein. The usual hangout was in the Uptown area between Hennepin and Lyndale avenues, along Lake Street. The pickings were all right, scouting out Doyle's Chicken Shack, Uptown Bowl, and going as far south as Porky's Drive-In. By the time we were seniors in high school, the familiar haunts were being taken over by gangs from the North Side, and their girls were just too mean to get involved with. The rich kids mostly came from the south suburbs of Richfield and Bloomington. The latter had a more lax law enforcement set up, and the girls were farm bred.

However, along with the passage of time comes change. The Highway 494 strip was host to hundreds of bars, hotels, shops, and now, the world famous Mall of America. By shear dead reckoning, I guided the Reliant through crowded neighborhoods looking for the Portman home on Clinton Avenue. With the note held in my finger tips to make sure I had the right house number, I hoped the Black Bear clerk gave me some straight dope. Pulling up to a small white rambler exactly like the small white ramblers set on either side of it, I matched the numbers on my wrinkled note.

Looking up at the house, other than the congestion of suburbia, the first thing I noticed was the front door standing half open. After so many years of doing what I did, I had developed a sense of what was around the next corner. Nothing good around this one. Slowly walking up to the open door, I could almost smell death inside. People who die in violence leave spirit sounds that are always more noisy than the casual heart attack. Their death is absolute and sudden. My foxy secretary, Jeanine, claimed to be able to hear the voices of victims of violent death. Which was one more reason to fear her. To me, the silence of death was a hauntingly muted and chilling presence of evil. Dull and dead. Nudging the door further open with my toe, I put my hand on the butt of the 9-mil strapped to my chest, hoping I didn't have to use it.

More sickened than surprised, as soon as I saw the carnage spread over the living room, I backed out and took out my cell phone. Sitting in the Plymouth, I waited about ten minutes before the street lit up like a carnival, red and blue lights gaily announcing a new attraction for the neighbors. I got out and leaned against the only fender on the Reliant that wasn't rusted, and waited.

A uniform trotted out to me, his .38 held down at his side. The first lesson any cop should learn was, don't assume anything and be suspicious of everything. "You call this in?"

"Yeah, I did."

"Turn around and put your hands on the vehicle please." A necessary routine I understood and obeyed. I was patted down, my gun and ID was taken, along with the contents from my pockets. I tried to see if the officer enjoyed toying in sensitive areas, but he seemed straight. Next came the cuffs. Another necessity to guarantee the officer's safety and the security of a possible suspect. Placed in the back of a squad car, I had an itch on my nose I couldn't do a thing about. The cuffs were grinding into my back and my arms were losing circulation.

About half an hour later, the door to the squad car opened. A squat man who looked like a derelict leaned in. His voice rattled, giving the impression that he was chewing on rocks. "C'mon, get out of there." Once outside, the cuffs were removed, and I was literally thrown against the side of the squad car. "We checked you out. Nobody in Duluth likes you. A Detective Grosslein said we could shoot you as long as you died."

Coaxing the blood back into my wrists and arms, I shrugged. "That's better than hanging me. Am I okay with you?"

The messy man in charge of this scene would be a respectable five-feet-eight if he stood up straight. His shirt hung out in back, and his fly was open. The sandy-gray on his head made him look like a rotting kiwi. The gristle hanging on his face did a poor job of hiding the pock marks and battle scars. I couldn't see if he was wearing a belt, as his stomach hid the top of his pants. I thought he could boil his shirt and make soup from the collection of garbage ground into it.

Sticking a wet stump that used to be a cheap cigar into his mouth, he growled, "Yeah, you're okay. We checked you out. You're just a gum-shoe sent out by the Duluth cops. Your friend Grosslein said he gave you a gratis job to get you out of the way." The messy man nodded toward the Portman house, "Looks like you hit the jackpot. We went through your car and found a confidential police report on a hooker and some stiffs. We heard about the politician that got iced, but that ain't none of our business. Yet."

He handed the file back to me, asking, "So, if you wanna get out of here unharmed, tell me why you got here. What has the Portman family got to do with the whore and the dead guys?"

I told the detective about Laura Blake picking up the unfortunate Donald to get away from the pimp following her. The bonds were none of his business, so I didn't mention them. "I'm assuming that this Billy Cummings killed the family trying to find his runaway prostitute." Lying the best I could, "I don't know why the whole family would get killed just for that. I was hired by the dead ambassador's wife to find him, and since this Blake woman seemed to be connected to his death I wanted to find her."

Detective Messy spit the cigar into the street. "Bruntz. I'm Detective Harold Bruntz. I want to be kept informed of anything you find. Understand?"

I got a cold chill thinking that Detective Messy Bruntz was bone-dead serious when he said something. There was a deeply sinister side to this man that I wanted not to annoy. "Yeah, sure. I'd appreciate some feedback on what this is all about to tell the Pierpont family."

A uniform trotted up to Bruntz and whispered into his cauliflower ear. He hoarsely muttered, "Oh, shit."

I caught the "there's more trouble" sign right away. "What is it?" I asked.

"There was a witness to the shooting. A different blood spot was on the carpet, one not near the massacred family, and there's a nine mil dug out of the door frame. I'm gonna keep your gun until we check for a match. I don't think it's yours, but I gotta be sure. Any questions?"

"Mind if I hang around?"

"Just don't get in the way." He pulled the handset from the squad car and barked, "Put out an APB on William Cummings and Laura Blake. Wake up the lab. I'm bringing in a blood sample and want a bullet marking comparison." He looked at me, turned his head and spit.

••••••••••••••••••••••••••••••

The day after the Portman family was discovered, a tall elegantly dressed Pamela Vanderguild accessed one of her safety deposit boxes, withdrawing five-hundred of the ten-thousand-dollar documents. The other drawer was left untouched. If anybody had made a crucial error, it was the bank assuming there was nothing unusual for a woman to cash five million dollars worth of bearer bonds. Struggling with a bulging duffel bag hanging from each shoulder, plus a huge handbag, the attractive well-dressed woman walked confidently out of the bank into the waiting Toyota. Carrie was perched nervously behind the wheel chain smoking. She took off as soon as Laura was seated.

Weaving through traffic, Carrie asked, "Any problems or questions?"

Ecstatic and giddy, Laura answered, "It was so fucking easy, girl. I just walked in and wham bam I was loaded up with cash. I could hardly walk out with all this shit." Letting a few glorious moments pass, Laura added, "Although . . ."

Worried at the cryptic comment, Carrie turned to her with a serious frown, "What? What do you mean *although*?"

Glancing over her shoulder at the bundles in the back seat, Laura told her, "There's more back there, babe. Some day when we know there's no trouble, we can come back for the rest." Turning back to Carrie, Laura smiled, "Five million, honey. We can get out and never take shit from anyone—ever."

Tingling, Carrie spouted a grin. "How many guys would we have to pork to earn that much?"

"You and me babe, we could do it during our lunch break."

Enthused, Carrie chortled, "Fuck 'em all, baby. I'm going to Switzerland or someplace. What are you going to do?"

Almost to their apartment, Laura's mood turned somber, telling her friend, "I've got some unfinished business before I go anywhere."

"Leave it alone, babe. You could kill Billy ten times over and still not make up for what he's done. I'll spend my whole life reliving what we had to do to stay alive."

Parked in front of the apartment, Laura turned to her and said, "I don't care. I want that prick to pay for wiping out that family. If it wasn't for me, they'd be alive. I don't give a shit if I die doing it. It's not the money anymore, Carrie. I'm going to do it. I'm going to kill Billy."

• •

Three weeks after the Portman family was slaughtered, the autopsy was done and the entire family was released to be buried. Forensics had dismantled their bodies enough to get all the information they could. Five closed caskets in a funeral paid for by Donald's employer. The complete family history had been withdrawn from relatives, friends, co-workers, and neighbors. There was not one single piece of information that led to any wrongdoing. Except for the credit card statement that Donald had paid for a prostitute at the Black Bear and the Travelodge. Considered a stupid move by his cohorts, it was accepted as a fling by a nerd to ease some mounting tensions. The fact that the prostitute was probably the cause of the murders, where she was just added to the mystery.

Since I was paid by the Pierpont family I felt I had a right to stay involved in the investigation. I was sure Grossy was glad to have me gone, so all I had to do was not piss off Detective Bruntz. I was surprised when I met his partner, a tall thin black woman who reminded me of one of those vibrating toys that bopped all over when wound up. I introduced myself. "Hi, I'm Norby Klein. I'm on assignment from the Duluth police department."

I held my hand out and was greeted with, "Who the fuck said you could muck up our investigation. Get away from me, you honkey shit. You ain't even a cop, mufuck."

Getting drop-kicked by Jeanine hurt less than that. I gave Detective Bruntz a pleading look and learned right then that he could smile and laugh. At me. Probably the only polite thing Bruntz had ever done was to introduce me to his partner. "Klein, meet Yo-yo Brown. Best partner I ever had." He gave her a smile that told me their relationship was a deep one. I respected that.

A stakeout was planned for the funeral. Photographers and plain-clothes spotters would be placed around the funeral home and cemetery. A photo of

Laura Blake was given to everyone, but from what I learned about the elusive woman, she was too smart to be seen.

I was not invited to sit in the car with Bruntz and Attila the black Hun, so I parked across the street in my Reliant, hoping I could catch any movement by the police if she was spotted.

• •

Sitting in his Cavalier in front of the funeral home, Yo-yo Brown asked, her partner, "Ain't we going inside?"

Bruntz, in his usual friendly growl, told her, "No, not yet. I want to see who shows up. I've got a camera crew taking pictures of everyone. I'm counting on that missing witness, or the hooker, coming out of curiosity. Whoever they are, they're either connected to the family or the killer. There's no report from hospitals, clinics, or doctors about a bullet wound. Someplace in this city there's a walking wounded that must be in a lot of hurt by now, unless they got some illicit quack to patch them up."

The two sat quietly exchanging small talk, Harold sipping his coffee laced with whiskey, and Yo-yo doing her nervous dance at the speed of sound. Harold's gut pressing against the steering wheel kept him from flopping forward, and Yo-yo started slipping down in the seat, doing the typical stakeout shuffle. From my spot across the street, I thought they were both sleeping.

Suddenly, the quiet slumber of boredom was violently shattered when Yo-yo jolted up, swinging her arm into Harold's face, shouting, "Holy shit, man, that's her. That's fuckin' her."

Harold's coffee and whiskey were now soaked into his shirt, running into the crotch of his pants. The two, scrambling in the front seat in a comedic routine to collect their wits, fell out of their respective doors to the ground. Hauling his body upright, Bruntz did the best he could to follow, not really certain why. I saw Yo-yo Brown dashing into the crowd milling at the door to the funeral home. Up on her tiptoes to scan over the heads of the crowd, she was craning her neck, but the target had disappeared.

Lumbering after his partner, Bruntz looked like a walrus that had peed in his pants, and was far too overweight to catch up.

Later, Yo-yo joined him at the door, stretching her neck to see over the crowd. "Son-of-a-bitch, man, she's gone."

Grabbing her arm, shoving her away from the spectators, he asked, "What, who?"

"That woman, you bonehead. The hooker I busted. They live together."

Me, being a highly trained professional, saw the fat detective and his skinny partner scramble in a Laurel and Hardy bit that had only one message. The witness had been spotted. Standing by my Reliant, I looked at the crowd and immediately saw the target. Two women stopped, turned, and ran. Hoping the Plymouth would start I climbed in, but I was cut off by a white Ford that obviously had the same idea I did. Follow the women.

Scrambling back to the Cavalier, Bruntz and Yo-yo Brown tried to get in line with the Toyota the girls had jumped into, a strange white Ford Galaxy, and my sputtering Reliant. More interested in the spectacle taking place in the street than the poor departed Portman family, the crowds gathered, yelling and pointing. Bruntz slapped a magnetized bubble to the top of the Cavalier but forgot to plug it in. They were stuck.

Frantic and jumping like a water bug, Yo-yo yelled at Bruntz, "Fuck the crowd, turn around, I know where they're going." Whipping a u-turn through the crowd, the two detectives fled in a flurry towards the apartment building on Humboldt Avenue. The cord to the still unplugged portable bubble was whipping in the wind outside the Cavalier as it wormed its way out of the milling gawkers.

• •

The Toyota raced through the streets to get back to the apartment before the expected crowd showed up. Carrie whined, "I told you not to go. We've been made."

Laura, trying to comfort her, said, "Don't worry. We'll get the cash and get out of here. I at least owed the poor man a visit at his funeral." Tears blurred her vision, as she lamented, "He died because of me. His whole family, Carrie. How can I live with that?"

"Just make sure we don't join them."

Out of control with the panicked Laura at the wheel, the Toyota jumped the curb in front of the Humboldt Avenue apartment, and died. The white Galaxy screeched to a stop behind it, smashing into the rear.

As I pulled up beside the mess, a tall greasy-haired dude was out and holding a gun at arm's length, running towards the two women. Everyone but me was screaming. So far. My turn would come very soon.

The greasy guy had to be Billy Cummings. The blonde woman was crouched holding her arms over her head as protection, and I didn't see the woman I assumed was Laura Blake. Before I could get my door open, I saw the pistol in Cummings's hand buck twice. The blonde lurched backwards and spurted blood as she dropped to the dirty turf.

Fortunately, Bruntz had returned my gun to me, and I had it pulled as I raced to the mayhem. It was then that I saw the other woman. She was screaming at Cummings, running to him with her teeth bared and claws stretching out. The most humane thing I could do was to shoot Cummings before the woman got to him. I planted a bullet into his shoulder, and he rolled over, his gun coming out, aimed at the screaming woman. The bullet grazed her cheek, spinning her back. I made the mistake of not realizing that Cummings was a killer, and I was his next target. I did a belly flop, the 9-mil from his gun parting the back of my head. I fired again, but I had no idea if I hit the bastard or not.

I assumed the dark-haired woman was Laura Blake. She was staggering, and her screaming had de-escalated to loud yelling. I brought my hand up to cover Billy Cummings, but for whatever reason, there was no gun in it. He was moving his body to face us, and all I really understood was, a) he was alive, and b) he was going to shoot us.

I grabbed the woman by the collar of her shirt and dragged her to the Reliant, which, thankfully, hadn't died or run out of gas. Pulling her to the driver's side, my classic Reliant became a shield. The windows splattered and the sheet metal ate bullets coming from Cummings's gun. He was on his feet, staggering to us. I saw him drop an empty clip on the ground only to ram in a new one. He was all set to start a new war. Something suddenly made him hunch over, and I used that miniscule moment to shove the woman into the

Plymouth and push her across the seat. The Reliant had all four cylinders howling like a cat in heat, putting a smoky oil screen behind us. The open driver's door hit a parked car and slammed shut, crunching my elbow.

About ten minutes too late, Harold's Cavalier careened off the curb in front of the apartment, landing next to the Toyota and the Galaxy. Yo-yo ran, while Harold waddled, up to the body of Billy Cummings. Kicking his gun away, Yo-yo crouched next to him, placing her fingers to his throat. Looking up with a frown of grief, she ceremoniously whispered, "Dead as a doornail."

Turning his body toward her, she pointed to the shoulder wound, and a bloody stub where his left ear used to be. Of a higher curiosity, she rolled him the other way and pointed to a larger blood-soaked hole in his back. She stood up, looked at Bruntz, and said, "The hole in his back's what killed him. It ain't the same caliber as the one in his shoulder."

Backing up, the two detectives scanned the neighborhood, but there wasn't a sign of anyone. Before the inevitable curious crowd showed up, they set up a perimeter and called in the ME and forensics team.

While the police were busy in the front of the apartment building, something else was happening in back. Two duffle bags filled with cash were being dragged out the rear door and piled into the back seat of a waiting car. As the investigators swarmed the building, the innocuous car quietly moved down the alley and disappeared into the traffic.

I had the Reliant calmed down now and took a moment to look at my passenger. Her head was leaning against the dirty head rest, an arm over her face. She was doing something I hated for women to do—she was crying.

When we got to the Lake Calhoun Parkway, I pulled over. I didn't dare turn off the Reliant, but it dieseled itself down anyway. As it was ticking to cool off, I asked the woman, "You're Laura?"

Surprised, she glanced at me with an "I give up look," sadly answering, "Yeah. How'd you know?"

I reached into the back seat and handed her the folder with all my information in it. Leafing through the pages, she tossed it back to me, adding, "Oh, shit. Now what."

Being suave and cryptic, I said, "I don't know, Laura. What *is* next?"

She reached for the door handle, yelping, "I gotta get out of here."

Gently pulling back on her arm, I gave her my logic. "You've got no place to go, and you're hurt. I'm assuming Billy Cummings is in custody, if not dead. I hit him in the shoulder, but that didn't keep him down. There was another shooter in front of the apartment. Billy was killed to keep him quiet. You aren't free yet, and I'm not sure the police are going to give you the protection you need."

The blood on her cheek had started to coagulate. Her eyes closed, I knew she understood everything. "Who are you? I know you aren't one of them. They'd never let you drive a piece-of-shit car like this."

Hoping my piece-of-shit Reliant didn't take offence at her comment, I said, "I'm a private detective hired by Elwood's wife to find him and the bonds. I'm assuming you have, or had, the bonds."

"Is that all you want? You're after all that green paper worth more than most countries? The money?" She looked at me. Her blood was soaking into my upholstery, and her face looked far from perfect at the moment, but I could tell why she turned on the ambassador. She was ten steps beyond gorgeous. Opening her lips, she spilled, "Know what they were to me? The bonds? Huh? Do ya? Freedom. To me and Carrie, they meant freedom from assholes who want nothing more than to have an orgasm and freedom from being slaves and get beaten for not sucking and fucking for them to become richer." Turning away, she lamented, "But now Carrie's free. All she wanted was to go home and not be embarrassed by men thinking they owned her."

The Reliant wasn't done ticking yet, so I sat awhile longer, then asked, "Where are the bonds, and no, I don't want them. My client does."

"We cashed half of them. It's all back in the apartment. If you're right about another shooter, I'm betting they're all gone now. Two bags filled with cash. Enough to feed hungry kids and send them to college." Looking back at me she hissed, "Satisfied?"

"Yeah, I'm satisfied. What about the other half?"

Smirking, her eyes still closed, "Put away."

My pocket started chirping, and I dug out my cell. "Yeah?"

The grinding voice on the other end was none other than Detective Harold Bruntz. "Where the hell are you? You got the girl?"

Not one prone to sarcasm, I said, "I'm fine, Detective Bruntz. I have a channel burrowed across the top of my head, but don't worry about me."

"Don't be a dipshit, Klein. Where's the girl?"

"Did you find my gun at the scene? I know I hit him once, then he gave me a haircut as I dove for safety. The girl's gone, Bruntz. By the time I got out of death's way, she'd booked. I cruised around but no sign of her. My guess is she's holed up with one of those families in the neighborhood that love cops."

"Fuck you, Klein. Yeah, we got your gun. Come in and get it."

Said the spider to the fly. I'm dumb, but not that stupid. "Thanks, old man. I'll be right in. Then you can tell me what you make of what went down."

In conclusion, Bruntz said, "Did you see another shooter?"

Bingo, I was right. "No. Another gun? No way."

"Fuck you, Klein. Get in here and make a statement." The disconnect was a relief. I didn't want an APB out on me. I wasn't sure if the Reliant could outrun a bicycle. That's if it would even start.

I was brought back to earth when I felt the warmth of a hand on my arm. Laura was looking at me, and said, "Thanks. Want to get the bonds?"

Surprised, I asked, "You sure? You trust me?"

"Yes, I'm sure, and, no, I don't trust you. I don't trust anyone, but don't have a lot of options, do I."

I needed to convince her she could trust me. I wanted the bonds, sure. Who wouldn't! But, there was too much blood on them. I got paid by the old lady, and I hoped she'd accept what was left of them. "No, your options are limited. You know I have to give them back to Mrs. Pierpont, don't you?"

Smirking, "That's a laugh. There not hers either."

Now, that woke me up. With as much intelligence as I could answer with, I said, "Huh?"

"Don't be naïve, Norbert."

"Call me Norby."

"Who, no matter how rich they are, carries all that value in a ten-dollar suitcase? What I overheard was that the bonds came from some Arab potentate. Elwood was supposed to negotiate a deal for nukes and small arms so a bunch of wild men to run around killing people. A small war was going to take place with all the death that went with it."

Quizzically, I asked, "How'd you learn that?"

Smiling, she told me what I already knew. "I get paid to listen, learn, and luxuriate men while they ravage me."

I hit the ignition key, forcing the Reliant to do something. It groaned, the engine rolled over a couple times, and coughed into life. I need to send a letter to Iacocca, or whoever turned out these babies. So cool.

I parked in the back lot of the Calhoun Beach Hotel thinking I could get us a room so we could deal with our wounds. Before I got out, Laura said, "Wait a minute. You look like shit."

"So, what's new?"

"You can't go in a place like this with blood caked on your head." She spit into her hand and started rubbing the sore on top of my head. Sounded gross and painful, but with a fox like that doing that to me, my mind was almost to the point of offering to pay her to do it more.

When she was done, I got a room. Back at the car, I reached under the seat and unclipped my spare .32 S&W. It had a full wheel, so I felt a wee bit safer. Laura was watching me but I had no idea what she was thinking.

CHAPTER TWELVE

THE ROOM WAS NICER THAN I DESERVED, but I figured Laura was accustomed to the fineries of sleeping accommodations. I had hoped to save water and take a shower with her, but wisely thought I should leave her alone. Gaining her trust was more important and demanded sacrifices. While that marvelous body was getting wet and soapy, by herself, I called Jeanine.

"Detective Grosslein called and said you're wanted in the Cities as a material witness. What the hell have you done now?"

"Oh, you know old Stu baby. He's just venting. I'm in Minneapolis and will try to get home tomorrow. If he calls again, say I went to Grand Marais, fishing. Be gone two weeks."

Disgusted, she hung up without saying goodbye, or that she loved me.

Everything I had, including the Smith & Wesson, were stuffed into my pockets. I was trying to earn Laura's trust, but I didn't trust her. The door to the bathroom opened with a gush of steam enveloping the woman. A towel wrapped around her body left her arms free to do something to her hair. It was at this point where I knew she was in control, like most beautiful women. She was a highly paid performer, specializing in making idiots out of men. The bottom of the towel came to about a centimeter below her magic garden. *"Oh, shit."*

Looking up from her hair business, she asked, "You say something?"

My tongue had softened enough to answer, "Uh, uhm, oh, ah."

"What? Speak up."

Shaking myself out of orbit, "Feel better? A hot shower always makes me feel better."

"Go ahead. Your turn."

As I stumbled into the bathroom, I saw her reaching for the wall-mounted complimentary hair dryer. Laura Blake might be a goddess in bed, or on my lap, or anywhere else, but in the bathroom she was a pig. The floor was puddled with water and the only dry towel left was the size of a pillow case. Stepping into the shower, I stared at the soap, imagining it had been rubbed all over her body. *"Oh, shit."*

Drying the best I could with the pillow case, I slipped into my boxers, but my feet were too wet to get into the legs of my pants. Taking a chance that I would appear modest, I crept into the bedroom. The sound of Dave Dahl giving the Channel Five weather report greeted me. Laura was partially covered by a sheet, one leg gracefully stretched over my side of the bed. My God, she was beautiful. My fantasy of smoothly talking her into a freebie was dashed—she was sound asleep. The not-too-large upholstered chair by the bed would have to be my bed for the night.

I woke up later with the outside safety lights partially illuminating the room. Dave Dahl had been turned off, and I was covered by a blanket. Laura had rolled over, showing me her million-dollar backside. Snoring. I fantasized for a while, then went back to my upholstered chair bed, instantly falling asleep.

I knew it was morning when the light in the room was different. Blinking, I looked over at the bed. The empty bed. Laura was gone. So was the door pass card, my wallet, and the four dollars I had left. I hadn't gotten dressed so fast since I was caught with the University of Duluth's librarian when her husband came home. He was the jerk who had chased me off the fire escape when I broke my foot. I couldn't find my shirt and was hobbled by my trousers around my ankles. Balancing against the bed, I heard the pass card open the door. The weight in my pants told me that my revolver was still in the pocket, and my car keys fell out, to the floor.

No worse, or better, than a kid caught with his young cousin, like I had been, I froze. Laura stepped into the room like she was conducting a tour of dignitaries through a museum. With a sparkle to her voice, she set the tray of coffee on the table and uncovered the doughnuts. Setting a large plastic bag on the bed, she handed me my credit card and wallet. "I forged your signature as Mrs. Klein, and bought some clothing in the gift shop. Mine was torn and bloody. I wore your shirt. Thanks. We'll pick up the bonds, and I'll pay you back."

Holding her new clothing up for inspection, she muttered, "The prices here are outrageous." Turning to me, she asked that mysterious question that no man on earth has an answer to, "Do you like this?"

"Uh, yeah. Looks fine."

She stripped off my shirt and my jaw fell to my knees as she stood half naked in front of me. She handed the shirt to me and asked a really dumb question. "Do I bother you?"

My voice reached a pubescent whine, "No shit, Laura. Yes, you bother me. Why wouldn't you? You're a babe and your naked. It was bad enough standing in the shower after you, then watching your ass while you slept."

"Sorry." That's all I heard before she was wrapped around me, taking me into space, twelve notches past the speed of light. *"This is Captain Kirk, Scotty. Do we have a reading?" "Aye Captain, you are being transformed into Play-Dough."* An hour later we were both in the shower this time. There were no dry towels so we rolled on the blanket in another marathon. Begging for resuscitation and a defibrillater, I slowly caught my breath while Laura bitched at me to get dressed.

The Reliant started again, and Laura returned my money, so I used my last four dollars to buy gas. Digging into her pocket, she handed me a twenty, "Here, don't be so cheap."

Back into the driver's seat, I started to say something, but she cut me off. "There's a dress shop. Pull over." She was out before the engine had died, disappearing into a trendy clothing store I wouldn't dare go near. Twenty-minutes later, she came out looking like an ad from *Elle*. A dark-blue power suit, high heels, hosiery, and smelled like an exotic recipe. Sunglasses worth more than my car sat on top of her well-groomed head.

"How did you pay for that? We're not going to be chased are we?"

Handing me my credit card, she scoffed, "Don't ask so many stupid questions. I can't go into the bank looking like a tramp. If the cops searched the apartment like they should have, they were certain to find some evidence that pointed to Fidelity Trust. They may be there ahead of us. What are you waiting for, get moving."

I put the credit card where I thought she couldn't find it, and pulled into traffic. Going back to my original question, I asked, "Where'd you get the twenty in the gas station?"

Her blasé answer, "I stole it from the gift shop."

Fidelity Trust had a parking ramp attached to it, so we hid the Reliant in a back corner. I insisted on going in with her to watch her back. Yes, her ass as well, but she needed another set of eyes. I had to leave the .32 in the car so we didn't set off any alarms. She took a deep breath, and told me, "If I get arrested, stay out of the way. Don't get made as I might need a connection outside if I'm taken."

I told her, "Wait a minute." I opened the trunk of the Plymouth and took a small plastic case back into the front seat. I handed her a tiny ear plug and showed her how to insert it into her ear. The trace along her cheek was obvious, but there was nothing to be done about it. I showed her my end of the mic, "You won't be able to talk to me, but you can hear me. If I see anything bad, I'll let you know. I'll direct you to alternate exits, if I can spot them."

Curious, she asked, "Where'd you get all the clandestine stuff?"

"I'm a private eye, honey. My job is to snoop where no man has snooped before. In strange bedrooms and beyond."

I think she smirked, but I couldn't be sure. She wiggled the receiver in her ear. I turned away and whispered into the mike, "Wanna go now?"

Smiling, she said, "Cool. I won't be able to cash the bonds. The bills would take too much room and raise too many questions if the bank has been alerted." She patted the large black purse, leaned over to me, giving me a warm wet kiss. "Let's go."

I had the mike strapped to my wrist, thinking I looked like the feds on *Criminal Minds*, carrying on conversations through imaginary wrist radios.

From the parking ramp we entered through an obscure door meant for cleaning crews and maintenance. Like she owned the frigging bank, Laura strode to the desk and asked for entrance to the safety deposit boxes. She signed her phony name and disappeared with the clerk. I snitched a ballpoint pen from a counter and unscrewed it, tossing out the ink cartridge and the top. Just a nervous suspicion I had. I held my wrist to my mouth, whispering, "So far so good. Stay calm and come out the same way you went in. Don't see any . . ."

I stopped when I saw the man leaning against a pillar outside the door to the safety deposit box closet. The tip off came from his demeanor and his shoes.

No cop on earth could, or would, dress like that. I don't know if he saw Laura go into the closet, but why would he be there in the first place? I talked to my wrist again, "There's a suspicious guy outside the door. He's not a cop. I'll run interference. You get out and get back to the car. You've got about three minutes before the shit hits the . . ."

Laura came out, half hidden by the large sunglasses, and the man stood up straight. I was right, he was a plant. She nodded to me ever so slightly and strode past him. The man turned to follow, and I stepped behind him, speaking into his ear. With the plastic pen body pressed into his back, I spoke, knowing Laura would hear me. "Don't even try it. Move to the elevators. Slow. That's it. You're smart and you'll live to tell your boss how you screwed this up. Don't look back, just move."

At the elevator door, I told him, "Press the button." Hoping there was nobody working with him, I pushed him through the open door and stepped in behind him. "If you want to die in an elevator just fuck up and I'll waste you here." I had his attention, but it wasn't going to last long.

I had him by a couple of inches in height and that was enough. I wrapped my arm around his neck and bulged my muscle as much as I could into his neck. I squeezed my forearm and bicep together, pressing his head forward. Hoping like hell I remembered how to do this without killing the guy, I set my feet to be ready for his struggle. What a woos. He went down like a hunk of meat. Holding on a moment longer than I should have, I punched the stop button, then went to the basement. I sent the elevator to the top floor and raced to the parking ramp. Yelling into my wrist, "Laura, I'm in the basement. Wait for me." My heart was screaming for mercy as I pounded my feet to try to reach the parking ramp before I died from a coronary.

I heard the sound but couldn't believe it was possible. I was right, it was the Reliant squealing down the ramp faster than it should have. I remembered that I had cut off the brake fluid to one of the rear wheels so I wouldn't have to fix a fluid leak. Laura, behind the wheel, didn't stop, but was nice enough to slow down so I could climb into the passenger seat. Panting like an old man after incredible sex, I was about to ask how she got the car started. When I saw the paperclip stuck into the ignition switch, I shut up.

Squealing out onto Marquette Avenue, the Reliant launched itself like an anemic spaceship. I started breathing again and held onto the door handle until my knuckles were white. I asked, "Where we going?" and saw the Highway 35 North sign whip past us. "Never mind." We were going home and that felt good.

CHAPTER THIRTEEN

● ●

AS LAURA MANEUVERED THE RELIANT NORTH on the freeway, my mind got tangled in all the questions I needed answers to. I received a warning from my bladder that I was about to have a problem. Approaching the Hinckley turn off, I pleaded, "I really gotta pee. Pull off here and take a left. Stop at Cassidy's and we can get something to eat." My legs were doing the pee-pee dance while I gritted my teeth.

With the skill of Danica Patrick at a NASCAR race, she wormed her way through the traffic lined up at the lights, returning comments from other drivers with the extension of her naughty finger. Into Cassidy's handicap parking spot, I was out the passenger door before she stopped, and flew to the men's room. There is no way to describe the relief when finally allowed to let go before the bladder takes charge and pushes harder than I can hold back.

I expected Laura to be waiting for me in the lobby of the restaurant, but I had been made a fool of before, so why not now. On my toes peering into the dinning room, there was no sign of her. "Oh shit."

Outside, I stood dumbly in the handi-cap spot where I thought she had landed. My disappointment in Laura was worse than the loss of my classic Reliant. I had twelve-cents in my pocket so a collect call to Jeanine for a rescue mission was my last hope. I picked my ego off the pavement to look for a phone, then I saw it. The Plymouth was parked in front of a White Castle, next door to Cassidy's.

Not in a mood to run anymore, I walked slowly to Laura, sitting in the driver's seat. My question was meant to be caustic. "You didn't like my choice of restaurants?"

"Shut up and get in."

I obeyed.

She pushed a bag of sliders to me and handed over a chocolate malt. Just the odor from the fried onion chips was enough to make me fall in love with her. Digging into the little cardboard slider holder, in my nonchalant manner, I said, "What the fuck are you doing?"

Her answer was one of those things women did to let us guys know we should just shut up and listen. More of a non-negotiable statement than an actual element of conversation. Jeanine did it to me all the time. "I didn't want to go into the other place. Okay?"

With a slider clamped between her teeth, she wheeled the Reliant around a pickup truck, and made her way back to the freeway. Thankfully, back in the right direction to go home.

A mile later she broke the silence. "I saw a guy walk into Cassidy's with his family, and I didn't want him to see me."

"A customer?"

"Yeah." More silence. I glanced over in time to see a tiny drop work its way down her cheek.

She reached over and squeezed my leg, telling me, "Thanks. I'd be dead if it weren't for you." Pulling off at the last rest area before Duluth, she shut down the engine and burst into tears. Damn. Why did women have to cry?

She got out, turned and said, "If you leave without me, I'll understand."

I watched her disappear into the women's bathroom and waited. No, I wouldn't leave without her. I looked in the back seat and saw the large purse filled with millions of dollars worth of bearer bonds. She trusted me.

She came back looking a little fresher. She opened the passenger door and said, "You drive." Settled in behind the wheel I sensed she wasn't done being emotional.

Folding one of those marvelous legs under her marvelous ass, she turned to face me. I ran my finger over the red track across her cheek. "Does it hurt?"

"It'll never hurt enough to justify what happened. I was responsible for that whole family getting killed. Carrie would have gone on working for Billy until she was too old. They're all dead."

I pulled the paper clip out of the ignition and put the key in. She wasn't done waxing yet, so I waited. I wanted to hear, and I knew she needed to unload, but it was killing me to listen. Looking at her, I saw my dead wife, Cheryl, and my dead lover, Marci. I wanted to hold her and make it all go away. I wanted to save her and make her safe and happy. I wanted her to stop having sex for money. I wanted her clean. None of that was going to happen.

"I hated what I was doing, Norby. I hated the way I was looked at. I was a piece of meat and available for whatever slime they wanted me to crawl in. I saw the bonds as a way out. I wanted to save Carrie, and was going to pay Donald back for everything. I made a promise to kill Billy for what he did to that family."

She looked deep into my eyes and I could feel the pain she was wrestling with. The flood came and she babbled through the storm, "I'm a whore, and I hate myself. I've destroyed so much, and I can't do anything about it." Clenching her fists, she wailed, "I'm a whore."

We stayed in the rest area until it was dark. She had her head in my lap, curled up like the little girl she had never been allowed to be, sleeping. A Winnebago pulled in, parking a few spots away from us. A woman came out of the side door carrying a baby into the bathroom. A man followed with a small boy attached to each hand. They forgot to close the camper door. Me, being the patron saint to saving lost and lonely souls, decided to wait until they came back to make sure nobody violated their privacy.

Laura woke up and sat upright. "What's going on?" I looked at her and fell in love. Her hair was hanging over the side of her face that held the red track, and was messy in an incredibly sexy way. Who could avoid falling in love with a vision like that. I was a stupid fool and knew it. All my life I had been my own fool, and now I was hers.

"Just a family taking their kids to the bathroom."

The family slowly walked back to the camper and all scrambled in. The inside lights went off, the engine started, and it slowly lumbered out of the rest area. I wasn't surprised by Laura's comment, "That's what I miss so much. Being a part of a family with kids and a husband who loved us all." She settled into the passenger seat, "Bullshit. Just another fantasy."

I eased the hair from her face, folding it over her head. Leaning in I kissed her and gave her my sage wisdom, "You and I are very much alike, Laura. I don't think much for fate, but it was by some plan that you and I wound up together."

She gave me that look again, kissed me back, and told me the truth, "Don't form attachments, Norby. Don't fall in love with me."

Now she tells me.

CHAPTER FOURTEEN

IT WAS AFTER MIDNIGHT AND DULUTH HAD SHUT DOWN. There was no place to go but my room on Superior Street. Not the best way to impress anybody, but our options were limited. Parking in front of the abandoned appliance store, I didn't lock the Reliant for two reasons. One, it wasn't worth stealing, and two, only one back door has a lock that worked. I found it comical that I was with a woman who had a purse filled with millions of dollars and we couldn't afford a decent hotel room. I could use my bank card, but I was really too cheap.

Holding the front door open for Laura, I had to guide her to my door. If more of the tenants would pay rent on time, management could buy a few light bulbs for the hallway. I couldn't complain. I was usually late too.

The caption under my high school year book photo read, *My memory is what I forget with.* I didn't have the greatest memory mostly because I didn't give a crap to store knowledge. When I put the key to my door lock, I instinctively turned the knob. It was unlocked. I'd be a fool to leave even my apartment unlocked in this neighborhood, but I couldn't specifically remember locking it.

When something isn't right, a special sense rings a bell. In my line of work, I'd be dead if I didn't have that little bell to tell me to be cautious. I slowly pushed the door open, and the hair on my arms bristled. Holding Laura back I slid in, my .32 held in front of me. Feeling confident that the revolver was all I needed to stem an attack. I ran my hand over the wall trying to find the light switch.

Click, click, click. No light.

I never felt the blow, but I'd remember the stars and hitting the floor for a long time. There were moments after that that seemed real and offered proof I was alive. But, I had no way to confirm it. My last thought was that I was going to die ingesting something off the floor of my apartment.

I'd been shot a few times, had my bell wrung more often, and suffered at the hands of those who pounded me with their fists. However, at this moment, I'd gladly go back and get my ass kicked again. My first recollection was a bright light. Stark white. Heaven? No, it hurts too much, and I didn't think I was heaven material. Voices? Not angels for sure.

The echo pounding through my head was ripping a path from ear to ear. "He's waking up." Ice cold water was tossed into my face, and I thought I was being water boarded. "Hey, Klein, wake up."

Slapping me was a bitchy thing to do, but it told me I was not in a hospital. I tried to bring my arms up to fight back, but they were either tied or had been cut off. More water and I got as pissed as I was scared.

I was bound to a flat surface, unable to move, and I had a hunch my death was going to hurt. I popped open one eyelid, and the bright light lasered through my head. "Oh, shit."

The voice behind me was deep and terrifying. "Good, you can talk. If you'd like to live another day, keep talking. If you don't talk, you die. Any questions?"

The most obvious question for me was to ask where I was, and would crying like a wimp help to let me go. Instead I thought I should play the game, if I knew what it was. Shakily, I asked, "What do you want?"

To the point with no misunderstanding of who had me or what they wanted. "The bonds, Mr. Klein. Where are the bonds?"

My stupid answer also told me to what lengths they were ready to go to get what they wanted. "What bonds?"

My body jolted and lurched against the restraints. I had never realized that so much pain could be followed by so much fear. "One-hundred-twenty volts, Mr. Klein. There's an alligator clip attached to your testicles, and one more pinching the end of your dick to complete the circuit."

It happened again, and now that I knew what it was, I launched into a new solar system where fear and pain were the only elements. It stopped, and my chest heaved with a cold sweat drenching me. Panting, I tried to talk. "The bonds, okay. Stop. Please stop and I'll tell you everything I know."

"Now we're getting somewhere. Go ahead, spill it."

Frantic about not blabbing too soon, I garbled the first words and had to start over. "The bonds." I had to pant enough to collect my story. "The woman at the apartment in the Cities. One was killed by Bill something. He was shooting at me, so I shot back. I didn't kill him, but he went down." I had to inhale and it sounded like a 747 taking off.

My mind was racing with desperation, trying to invent something plausible. "The woman ran to me and I pushed her into the car. When that guy went down, I saw a chance to get away. I took off. The woman was yelling at me. She said . . . she said we had to go back and get something. I told her we were alive and that was enough. She screamed that she had to go back. Later, I pulled over. Told her to tell me . . . to tell me what was going on. She told me about the bonds. They were at the apartment, and we had to go back. I told her she could do anything she wanted, but I was going home."

I was hyperventilating and thought about the clamps attached to my pride and sometimes joy. "She . . . she was crying. Said her friend was dead and the bonds were gone."

The voice again, "Why were you there at all, Mr. Klein?"

"Mrs. Pierpont hired me to find a package her husband had. Didn't tell me what. He was killed in Duluth. I followed that Donald guy the whore seduced, thinking the woman had the package. Found the bodies of Donald and his whole family and went with the cops to the funeral. They saw the woman but got hemmed in. I followed her. That's when the shooting started. That's all I know. The woman's gone and I don't know, or give a shit for the bonds."

The murmuring voices seemed to come from all over wherever I was. There was some rustling and I heard the slide of a pistol injecting a bullet into a gun chamber. The explosion was the last thing I heard, and I said goodbye to Cheryl. There was no time to apologize again.

To say I felt like shit would be a gross understatement. I could move my arms and wiggle my toes, but everything else was dead. So, I was kind of alive—maybe. The soft hand on my arm and the rasping sound of Velcro on a blood pressure cuff were reality.

I had my arms, my toes, and blood pressure. It was a beginning. The voice made me jump, thinking I was going to light up again. "Mr. Klein, I'm glad to see you coming around." The cold stethoscope was a good sign also. "You were put through some harrowing ordeals, but I was told you were too tough to give in to a little electrocution and a bullet in your head. I'll be back later to see how you're doing. There's someone here to see you."

Bullet in my head?

The familiar and grating voice of Detective Stuart Grosslein was a welcome intrusion. "Hi, Grossy. You missed a swell party, man."

"Maybe next time. You can let me do the electric stuff. Jesus, Klein, what the fuck did you get into? I sent you out to talk to a hotel clerk."

Now I knew he loved me.

He pushed me over so I almost fell off the other side of the bed and sat next to me. I was impressed with his touchy-feely side. We talked about an hour covering the last few days, and I told him everything. Except about Laura. I let him believe I lost her in Minneapolis.

The doctor came back after Grossy was done rattling me. My personal area was fried, and it might hurt awhile, but with ointment and care, I'd be good again. I was never good in the first place, so that was good news. The bright spot was when the nurse came in to apply the ointment. At least one other function worked. Oh, yeah.

The bullet had hit my thick skull and was diverted to the outer surface of the brain.

Any closer and I'd be hanging out with Hanky begging for muscatel.

The bright part of my day came in the form of my secretary, Jeanine. Tight-fitting jeans and a loose tank top were enough to stress my burn, requiring another ointment treatment. She comforted me by telling me that she had taken on a few cases herself and brought in a few bucks. I had her close the door and told her all about Laura and the bonds.

I never questioned how I was found, but she told me, "The police received an anonymous call that the cops were needed at some address in a warehouse near the edge of town. It was a woman, and she put enough of a spin on it to get them to hurry."

"Laura." When I was cold-cocked in my apartment, she must have taken off. Jeannine said my car had disappeared, so I'm assuming Laura found another paper clip and followed whoever to wherever. At least she was still around.

I told Jeanine, "We have to find her. Somebody's going to kill her."

Her understanding and cooperative attitude came out when she said, "What's this *we* shit."

• •

I spent my recovery period sitting in the kitchen of HellBurger, looking like a mummy with my head wrapped in white gauze. I limped and the ointment helped, but not as much as when the nurse applied it. In a couple weeks I knew I was healthy again when I could belt down a shot of Old Mr. Boston without getting a headache and barfing. When I threw up in Mitch Omer's kitchen, he really got pissed. The first time he chased me through Canal Park with a meat cleaver. My recovery went smoother when I could sit out front at the bar with real patrons, as long as I could pay and didn't vomit.

The overriding thought that carried me from one miserable day to the next was wondering where Laura was. I knew she cared a little bit because she was following the bad guys, and then reporting it, but she still hadn't shown up. My best guess was that she had taken my Reliant back to the Cities, or wherever. I knew it wouldn't get her too far.

Also, I had some unfinished business with Adelle Pierpont. I had hoped to bring at least half the bonds back, but chances of that looked pretty slim. A couple of weeks later, nearing the idea that I couldn't avoid reporting to the old lady, my world took another turn. Dragging myself home from a day at HellBurger, getting wasted, I stopped and stared at my Reliant sitting in front of the apartment.

Chapter Fifteen

● ● ● ● ● ● ● ● ● ● ● ● ● ● ● ● ● ● ● ●

THERE WAS SOMETHING STRANGE ABOUT MY CAR. It had a distinct smell that was new to me. I felt around inside and it was clean. No, I really mean clean. The floor had been vacuumed, and the shot-out windows were replaced. Then the strange smell hit me. In the darkness on Superior Street, I fumbled my way to the front of the car and felt a tire. Stunned, it was new. I was smelling the nauseating sweet odor of four new tires.

Profoundly thrilled, I backed away from the car, eager to take it for a spin. I backed into a solid body behind me. I froze. I was dead certain my torture friends had come back. If my .32 was someplace, it was not with me. In no shape to fight or argue, I considered screaming and running.

Then a familiar bony hand clenched my shoulder, and my fears turned to joy. "Hanky, you gotta make some noise, man." I gasped. "I'm too old and fucked up to be scared like that." I gave Hanky's skeletal body a man-hug and shook his hand to let him know I loved him.

"Hanky, who put my car here? Did you see?" I could see his yellow teeth in the darkness and assumed he was smiling.

From deep in his body someplace, a voice wheezed out his mouth hole. "Woman put it there."

"A woman?" It was either Laura or Jeanine. I knew Jeanine's limits and there were many things she would never do. Sleeping with me would only happen in my dreams, and I was pretty sure she would never put new tires on a car she refused to drive. Or ride in. So, that left Laura as the most logical person to bother to buy tires for my piece-of-shit relic.

Hanky gurgled, "Pretty. Smell-good woman."

Handing him my last ten, I said "Thanks, buddy. Some day, Hanky, I'm gonna get you laid. I think you could use it. I just have to find the right, um, person."

He pocketed the ten and slid into the darkness. I was anxious to get upstairs, but cautious. The last time I turned into a light bulb and took a slug. Working my way to the rear of the building I crept upstairs, slowly, listening. Sliding along the wall to my room, I had no idea how I was going to open the door safely.

Tonight might as well be Halloween for all the scary contacts I made. First Hanky, now a new one. It was pure premonition and gut I felt. Then, I smelled it. Better than new tires, it was like some spiritual flower that had essence rather than odor. She stepped from the shadows, floated to me, and put her arms around my neck. I still couldn't see her, but the soft wet heat coming from her mouth turned me to butter being poured over naked flesh. Laura. Who else could do that in real life?

She spoke into my mouth, "It's safe to go in."

When she said, *go in*, my fantasy shot out of control. Of course she meant the room. My room. The door closed behind me, and I heard the bolt slide shut. The shades had all been pulled down, even the torn one. I reached for the lamp, but she took my hand, pressing it to her lips, and whispered. "No lights. No one can know we're here." A match scratched and flared, igniting a blue candle I had never seen before.

The flickering glow on her face did it all over again. The dark hair framing her, a silk blouse and short skirt clothing that sleek body. The skirt dropped first, then the blouse floated away. That was all. My clothes evaporated, and we stood together, entwined. Her body was on the edge of being hot. Soft, super warm, and smooth. Her lips tasted far better than the White Castle onion chips.

I had no illusions about my ever being good enough to go to heaven, but now I didn't need to. Where I was had to be on the cloud that nobody else knew about. Floating in and out of sensual pleasures, mind numbing orgasms and more soft flesh. The magic garden had opened for me, and I went in. Hot, moist, sweet, a heaven of its own.

The candle burned down, spewing its waste on a chair next to the bed. The glow on absolute perfection, mounds of breasts peaked by the erect statue, her flesh flowing down her body, no interruption by hair, anywhere. The only thing spoiling this trip of erotic magic was on the chair next to the candle. A

Colt .45 pistol, made longer by the silencer attached to the death end of it. Knowing Laura, and about Laura, I was willing to place a bet that the slugs were hollow point. At close range, one of the deadliest weapons that could fit in a hand. Even the small soft, sensuous hand, that was performing miracles on the charred remains of my manhood.

I woke up in the morning with a better outlook on a shitty life. She was still here, and still warm and soft. The gun was gone, and when she saw me look at the chair, she pulled it out from under her pillow. I dropped the clip, and I was right. Hollow point. Giving it back to her, I asked my first dumb question, "You sure you need that?"

Her comment illustrated how stupid I was. "You're a real bone head, you know?" she said. "Yes, I need this. If I could fit a flamethrower in my purse I have one of those also. When you went down the last time, I knew I'd be dead in a heartbeat. You too. When they have the bonds, they have no need for us. No more than they did for the Portman family, or even Billy himself. They knew where the cash was and everyone else was expendable."

"Cash?"

"Yeah, cash. Carrie and I had two duffle bags filled with millions in raw cold cash. The cops never found anything in the apartment, so while the OK Corral was going on in front of the apartment, they were inside taking the dough."

"You cashed them in?"

"Duh! We were on our way to San Jose, dude. One way trip with enough cash to keep going. My mistake was getting choked up over the Portmans and insisted we go to the funeral. Wow, what a mistake."

"And now you have the other half of the bonds. You do, don't you?"

"Don't worry about the bonds, sweetie. Yes, I have them, and no, they cannot be had, by anyone but me."

"Laura, is it worth the possibility of your getting nabbed by these people and forced to tell them? They're professional enough to consider killing you anyway if you don't give them up. If they can't have them, neither can you."

There was a long silence, but I doubted she was weighing my logic. Laura Blake was the absolute smartest woman to ever commit a crime. I cannot afford to underestimate her resources and expect to live. Or make out with her again. When she spoke, I knew I had underestimated her. "I know who killed Elwood Pierpont. I helped them do it. If I hadn't, they would have killed me that night, too. The same person killed the driver that night. They are also driving the people who tortured you. Those guys are just messengers, Norby. I sent word to them that if I was harmed in any way, the bonds and proof of who they are will be made public."

Exhaling my frustration, I asked, "Did you possibly mention me in that note? That I wasn't to be hurt?"

"Oh, sorry. I forgot."

I was against the wall here and possibly in more trouble than my murdering lover. Hoping to work on her humanistic side, "Laura, sweetheart, I need to give those bonds back to Adelle Pierpont. Is there any way for that to happen? That's more money than the pope has, honey. Why not slip one or two out for yourself and give the rest back. I don't want any of it. You can keep it all."

Her hesitation scared the crap out of me, and I pictured myself becoming another electrical conductor. When she spoke I knew I was outclassed. "I have something for you." She dragged that large purse to her and drew out one of the precious pieces of green scrolled paper. Opening the bag she showed that there were no more. "Bring this to the old lady. Tell her I'll make a deal, and she can tell the syndicate to back off and go away for good."

"Syndicate? How deep does this go?"

"You know where the bonds come from. The Arab that was buying arms is going to put pressure on the syndicate. Which is why I want to deal and get out. Fast."

"What kind of deal?"

"I'll take ten of the bonds."

Now I was really getting confused. "Is Adelle Pierpont involved with this syndicate?"

She started getting dressed. "Her husband was, but I'm not sure she's in it."

Before she left, she turned and said, "I'll get back to you after you see the old lady. And, by the way, your car is a piece of crap, but I made it special for you. Don't get rid of it. However, I knew I'd never get it back here until I put tires on it. There's a nice lake out there. Get a boat." And as an afterthought, I wouldn't catch the meaning to until much later, she said, "Get a boat, yeah, but keep the car."

Chapter Sixteen

My Reliant stood rather proudly under the Pierpont portico, new tires and all. I bet Kathleen would even ride in it with me now that the empty McDonalds bags were gone. It was too late for visiting anyone, but when I called, the beautiful Kathleen told me to come over anyway.

It was a chilly night with a cool breeze coming off the lake. I wished someone would open the door before hypothermia set in. People in Minnesota should wear down jackets all the time. I saw the shadow move across the tiny window set into the door. If it was Kathleen again, I'll ask her to warm me up.

The huge door opened to reveal a vision that even made Laura look like a dragon. She lingered long enough for my body temperature to drop another degree in the wind, all while my blood reached the boiling point. Beige again. This time it was soft and fluttered from the breeze wafting through the open door. Evidently, it was some kind of bed wrap with no buttons or ties. I didn't care what mystery caused it to cling to her body, only if it would come off easily. Those amazing arms were bare, and just now, I noticed a slight triceps muscle flex as she moved.

The wrap draped to the floor, and she was barefoot inside of it. One other mesmerizing feature was her nipples. She had worn her nipples tonight and they were trying to talk to me. Pencil eraser hard, long, and dark pink. How much of this was I supposed to endure? Did she understand that I was more than a sex symbol?

"Uh, hi, Kathleen."

Stepping aside, she whispered, "Come in." The door closed behind us. When she ran her hand across my back, I had an idea just where this was going. "This way." And, like a programmed robot, I followed. The ethereal way she moved held a message that I was too human to understand. The hair, soft gold, long and flowing, was enticing enough, but through the shear fabric caressing her rear, I wanted to stick my face into the cleavage between those marvelous mounds us mortals call an ass.

We were transported to her bed room where another Olympic marathon took place. Sometime during the night, I managed to wheeze out, "Any chance I could see your mother?"

As she buried my face in one of her special places, I heard, "In the morning."

Morning finally did show up, and I was exhausted. Kathleen was nowhere in sight, and there was no sound, other than my own panting. Peeking into the bathroom, my hopes were dashed. Empty. I squeezed out my morning fluid, hoping to not spray the sterile-looking floor. A cursory scan of the medicine chest gave up a collection of meds ranging from, Abilify, Viibryo, Prozac, Fevarin, Ambien, Lunesta, all the way to Saphris. Now, I wasn't a pharmacist but I knew enough about drugs to get a picture. The seductive mistress of the Pierpont Manor was an oversexed, depressed, schizophrenic insomniac. I could attest to the oversexed part, but I was surprised at the rest. Of particular interest was an outdated supply of birth control pills. It was tucked way in the back, so getting knocked up was not a problem now.

Remembering to flush, I collected my clothing, strewn across the room, and became decent again. Still messy, but decent. I managed to find the dining room by following the scent of food. The sideboard was replete with silver serving dishes, and most obvious, a large coffee urn. At one end of a long mahogany table sat the mother superior, staring at me. Unsure of being invited, I hovered, trying to smile.

The raspy voice carried well across the table, and was frightening. "Oh, for Christ sake, Mr. Klein, get some breakfast and sit down."

Like a kid in a toy store, I lifted the lid on each container and filled my plate. I sat. Gorging myself, I hid my burp, but the gas escaped before I could squeeze it back in. On cue, a uniformed maid took my plate away and set a fresh cup of coffee in front of me. I realized that the old lady had been watching me, and I assumed, scrutinizing what her hundred grand had bought.

Trying to relax, she started the conversation, making me more nervous. "If you are done, let's get to it. You have less than good news for me, don't you."

What was left to say? "It depends on how you look at it, I suppose. Yes, I have about half of the bonds. The rest had already been turned into cash and stolen by the syndicate your husband was involved in. I have a hunch the cash isn't too far away." I left that hang, hoping for a response. She was too smart to get trapped.

"The bonds. Where are they?"

I pulled out the bond Laura gave me, laying it on the table. Her face got hard and she sneered, "Where are the rest?"

"The woman who your husband was with has them. She wants to make a deal for the rest."

The old woman lifted her cane and pointed it at me. She clenched the silver, knurled handle tightly in her bony fist. Her voice came out in a hiss that could melt glass, "Do you know what happened to the last person who tried to blackmail me? Their remains are nourishing the bottom feeders. Shreds of their flesh float as fodder for the stupid animates that have no meaning."

Shifting in my chair, I toyed with my cup, trying to find an answer. She didn't give me enough time, and my brain was running out of ideas. "You go back and tell the whore that I *will* have the bonds, either by them being given to me—or taken back by force."

I shouldn't have been surprised she knew so much. "You . . . ?"

"Laura Blake is a clever and cunning woman. She's smart enough to realize that if she tries to screw me, she'll hurt terribly." The sample bond slid under her hand, and I didn't dare reach for it.

Before I got to the door, her voice nailed me in the back. "If you keep fucking my daughter and Laura Blake you will kill yourself." A clever and entertaining thought, but the reality of her meaning hit me hard. Then she snapped at me, "And, if you don't quit fucking my daughter, I'll kill you. Understand?"

The Reliant started, and while it vibrated under the portico, I counted my blessings thinking that I was lucky to have come out of the conversation with Adelle, alive.

I looked for a parking spot near the police station. I knew I was over my head and needed to clean out some of the garbage. I needed to find out what Grossy had and if I was in trouble with him. Just seeing the scowl on his face, I knew I was in deep shit.

Sitting uninvited at his desk, I listened as he ranted. "So, I get this call from some city cop that my ... *associate* had a file with more information than anyone needed." He took time to lean into my face and scream, "The fucking files you copied from my desk." He went from the hands-on-hip stance to a pulling-out-hair routine to express himself.

During a lull in his tantrum, I asked, "They have my gun. Can you get it back?"

I had been tossed out of bars all my life. I'd been kicked out of ball games, card games, pool halls, whore houses, and now, for a first, I was tossed out of a police station. I was usually dragged into one. Collecting my pride, I scanned the parking ticket under the wiper blade, dismissed the idea of getting Grossy to erase it. Looking back at the wiper blade, I saw it was in shreds against the windshield.

I had no idea where to find Laura, thinking that maybe Mitch Omer knew of a haunt she might hide in. Walking through the kitchen of HellBurger, I saw Pappy arranging stuff behind the bar. Looking up, he greeted me with a usual, "What the fuck do you want?"

"I love you too, Pappy. Mitch in his office?"

"Yeah. Tell him to choke or poison you. I don't wanna clean up no bloody mess from a gun or knife."

"I appreciate your concern." Walking down the dark hallway, I rapped on the door after I had it open. Mitch was sitting with Cynthia, his lifelong love and guardian. Mitch growled, but Cynthia gave me a smile and a warm kiss. She touched the red spot on my forehead where the bullet hit.

Pushing herself away, she had to ask, "How they hangin', Norbs?" Her caustic smile told me that the reference was to my boys being fried.

As she left, I said, "They still work."

Taking my place next to Mitch, I started talking before he had a chance to reach for a weapon. "I lost the girl, Mitch. Laura. She's in a lot of trouble, and I gotta find her."

I didn't want him to pontificate over how stupid I was, but I was surprised by getting some sage advice instead. "She's a whore, Norbs. Let her go. I've seen her work, and there's no one better. I got all the news on the pimp and some of the shit that went down. I don't want to know any more. It's a bad crowd. From what I gather, they're going to tear this town apart looking for her."

"Any idea where she might find safety?"

"Not anymore. My guess is, she's gone. Whatever it is that's making her so hot went with her."

I doubted that, but I kept my mouth shut on it. I had another problem. "I need a gun."

He scooted his chair to the door and swung it shut. "I got a Ruger p95. A 9-mil and it's not even hot. Five bills, with three full clips."

I accepted, then argued for ten minutes, but he relented. "Fine. I'll have it drilled and tapped for a silencer. Another grand."

"Do you take credit cards?"

CHAPTER SEVENTEEN

THE RUGER WAS EXPENSIVE BUT EASY TO GET. Nested in a leather holster in the small of my back, I had to wear a jacket to cover it. It was late now, and I didn't have a clue what to do next. The old lady was waiting for her bonds, I was waiting for Laura, and I had a hunch the syndicate was waiting for me. I sat in the Reliant down by the lake until it was murky enough to move around.

Parking a couple blocks away, I crept through the shadows up Superior Street. If I hung around long enough, Hanky was sure to come up behind me with a potential heart attack waiting. It was amazing how predictable some things were. Yes, he did sneak up on me, and yes, I was certain I was going into cardiac arrest when his hand touched my shoulder. I shuddered to think of Hanky giving me mouth to mouth.

Panting, I said, "Jesus, Hanky, give me some warning." Collecting myself and reassuring him he was still my best friend, I asked, "Did you see the woman? The pretty one?"

I'm certain I saw his head move with a shoulder shrug, meaning he didn't know. Fishing for more, "Anyone else come around?"

Now I hit pay dirt. He pointed up to my room, rasping out, "Bad men. Up there."

Oh shit. "How many?"

His trembling hand held up three fingers.

Appreciating what he was giving me, I wanted him out of the way if some bad crap came down. "Thanks, buddy. Now you have to disappear. If the shit hits the fan up there, this place will be crawling with cops." I also knew that if the cops didn't show up, I'd be ass deep in bad guys.

I turned away to check the security on the street. Twisting back to make sure Hanky was safe, he had done what I'd asked, and disappeared. I was alone.

I felt like the Pink Panther sneaking down the alley behind my apartment. Crouched in a dark corner, I reached back for the Ruger and threaded the silencer into place on the muzzle. Too long now, but essential. The three goons in my building were waiting for both me and Laura, and I had no idea how they were set up.

Logic would put one as a lookout downstairs, one outside the apartment, and the last one inside the room. The window to the furnace room was never locked. It was cheaper to keep it open for the bums to get in on cold nights, than it was to keep replacing glass. Silence was my only weapon right now. I needed to cram my fat ass through the furnace room window, not making a sound. And, if one of them was posted in or near the furnace room, I was dead.

I saw drunks and derelicts going through this window all the time. This was no place for a middle-aged overweight lazy man to be, and I kept having this idea about getting shot again once I was inside. This was nuts. I lived here, so what the hell was I doing. With a final push and huff, I farted, and I was in. The only glitch was ripping my pants on the window sill. Peering out the door to the basement, all I heard was my own heart pumping like an oil rig. I knew this basement well. I had to hide down here a few times. Up the steps to the back of the building, I got to the first floor hallway. Dark as an armpit, I was now in the back trying to sense some kind of life someplace.

The idiot stationed by the front entrance did what any idiot would do while hiding in the dark, he lit a cigarette. What a dip-shit. The flare from the match lit up the hallway like a stage play. The scary part of his stupidity was the confidence he had in being so obvious.

I didn't want to be here, but if Laura was upstairs, I needed to get up there. I could just leave and live, but that wasn't going to happen. All I needed was a white horse and some armor. I leveled the Ruger at the glow from the cigarette but had to lower the weapon to stop shaking. Again, I pulled the gun up and waited for him to take a drag.

The glow from the tip lit his face, and I had to squelch the idea that he was a human and didn't deserve to die. Bullshit. He was here to kill me. I sighted, held my breath, and squeezed. *Pht.* He yelped and his body crashed into the stair railing, breaking something and staggered to the front door. He fell, his body half in, half out of the doorway.

When two guys suddenly crammed into the door from the outside, and one more came stomping down the steps, followed by shouting from upstairs, I knew I was outmatched, outgunned, outmanned, and outsmarted. My only option was to creep back into the basement and hide.

The commotion upstairs escalated. Men yelled, and then all went quiet. Settling back into the spider webs, I sat on the cold dirty floor trying to catch my breath. When the shaking and cold sweats stopped, I propped the Ruger on my knees and went to sleep.

Years later, looking back on this scene, I regretted not leaving and never going back. I should have crawled out the furnace room window and learned to live with Hanky. The thought was chilling, but made more sense.

I knew it was morning when my bones started screaming to be put back into place. Stumbling out of my corner, I had to wipe the spider webs away from my face. I couldn't stand up for a while, but with determination and accepting the pain, I became a human again.

Cautiously, I made my way back up to the hallway. At the front door, I saw that the railing to the stair was broken, the screen to the entry door lay in the street, and there was a trace of blood streaking across the sill of the door. He must have lived, or they would have left him there.

The creaking of the stairs sounded like a fire alarm with each step I took. Passing Mrs. Feldstein's apartment, I heard the door knob turn and lowered the gun to my side. The last thing I wanted was for her to come blasting out of her apartment to get the guy with a gun. And, another last thing I wanted was for her to get in the way.

The door cracked enough to see the Spoolie-infested gray hair through the crack. She pre-empted my thinking of how to push her back into the room by nodding to me and cranking her head to the side. She was telling me there was someone in my apartment.

Sliding along the wall, I inched to my door. It was ajar about an inch. Oh, shit. Now what? How did I get here? How badly do I want to go in there? I put my toe against the bottom of the door and nudged it open a few more inches.

No sound, no movement, nothing. However, that meant nothing. Open a little more, see what I could, and lead with the Ruger. I had taken the silencer off, giving me a lot more agility with it as my point guard. My left foot over the threshold, I moved my body in more, but all I could see was the door to my bedroom, past the kitchen. I wondered if the turds were still in the coffee pot.

The apartment was small enough to see that nobody was anywhere that I could see. The only place left was the bedroom, and that was small enough to make a crowd out of two people. The striped ticking of the mattress came into view, then the headboard, and then the flood of blood draining over the side to puddle on the floor.

"Aw, no." Laura's beautiful arms were tied behind her and her feet were bound. Her clothing was torn and the bed was torn apart. She'd put up a struggle, but not enough. Her head was hanging over the side, eyes wide open staring at nothing, her mouth gaping. That soft smooth throat I had so wantonly kissed and caressed was open and yawning. The pink and red parts that held her head in place were falling out of the gash, held in place by the coagulating blood.

I had no idea what happened to the gun that got me this far. Stupidly and blindly, I stumbled to the bed, reaching out to touch that mane of hair that had brushed my face when she made love to me. Through the tears and anguish I slobbered, "Oh, God, no."

I sensed they were behind me, but my grief had overwhelmed my actions. I didn't see it come over my head, but as the thin leather strap dug into my neck, I knew I was going to die. Horribly. The fear was worse than the pain. I thought it was going to pull right through my neck and sever my head. I'd take another shot of voltage to my package rather than the searing white hot pain paralyzing me. It was happening quickly, and my struggling and the frantic waving of my arms only made it worse.

I've never been know as a quick thinker, or even very smart. In a flash of sanity that was stronger than my fear and the pain, I willed my body to become limp, dropping to the floor like a rag. The fun for my attacker must have been over when I did that because the leather garrote was stripped from my neck. I could feel my flesh rip off with it. I needed to play dead, which was easy, as I was quickly passing out.

In the infinitesimal moment before my entire system shut down, my head on the floor lying in the puddle of Laura's blood, I saw it. On the floor, in front of my eyes was the murder weapon. And the puzzle began to assemble itself.

Chapter Eighteen

UNFORTUNATELY, I WAS ALIVE, BUT TO WHAT EXTENT was yet to be seen. The room was dark or my eyes were closed. I didn't know which. I tried to lift my hand. Another hand held it in place. A warm soft hand that welcomed me home to the land of the living. I could feel the callouses on it that had hurled a softball at the speed of light, and had splintered a board and smashed a brick. The same hand that had crippled me when I made a pass at her.

I opened my lips and rasped, "Jeanine."

Her soft melodic voice welcomed me, "You dipshit. What the fuck were you thinking? Oh, I know, you weren't. Why did you go there alone? Nobody walks into a murder scene without back-up. You dipshit. Jesus, I don't believe it."

Understanding her being upset, I asked, "Will you have sex with me?"

Her response was sharp and to the point. "Yeah, I will. I'll let you bong every opening I have on the very day you become smart."

I knew that would never happen.

She left me in good spirits, replaced by a pit bull in a white uniform adorned with a stethoscope hanging around her ample neck. This one would scare Charles Manson. I didn't get a look at her name tag, so I assumed it was either Warkill, or Attila the Hun. In my most congenial voice, full of static, I asked, "Can I go home now?"

I knew I had charmed her and she loved me. "Shut up. You're not supposed to talk. The doctor will be in soon." Watching her do a goose step out of the room, I imagined the doctor she was referring to might be called, Doctor Mengele. In truth, the doctor was very nice, explaining that I had suffered severe damage to my throat and needed surgery to put me back into my usual sylphlike shape.

I was out of the hospital two weeks later with my throat wrapped with what I thought looked like feminine napkins. There was no way I could force myself to go back to the old apartment. Jeanine put me up for another week, but I guess my presence was too much of a strain on her sexuality. She had a bed put in my office and told me to get out.

I was grilled by the police, who seemed to want to say I was guilty of murder. They found the body of a guy and the 9-mil dug out of him matched the Ruger I had dropped in my bedroom. I paid a lawyer too much to convince them that it was self-defense. I was back in Grossy's good graces again, but since I couldn't, and wouldn't, tell him any more about Laura, he told me to get out and never come back.

The autopsy on Laura showed she had been tortured before her throat was slit. A familiar pattern with the alligator clips to her breasts and electrocuted. I wanted to throw up. If she had given up the bonds it would have been a blessing, but I didn't think that happened. What they did to her was pointless. There was no reason for it. I filed the picture of her lying on the bed, her throat … oh, shit. I put the whole scene away in the back of my mind as a stimulus to be used later. I had a score to settle and needed to get really pissed before I did anything about it.

Her body was buried in an obscure spot in Union Cemetery, between Hermantown and Proctor. I popped for a small headstone, thinking she deserved at least that. She'd had a hard life and suffered a hard death, but my inner feelings told me I wasn't done with her yet. The only picture of her I had was the mug shot, which didn't do her justice. No camera could. I entertain myself now by looking at the pictures of the three women who had impacted me the most. My wife, Cheryl, Marci Hudson, and Laura Blake. I was in love with all of them, but only held one in my heart. I cried myself to sleep, hoping I wouldn't wake up, but my punishment wasn't over yet, and I faced another morning.

The bourbon tasted better sitting at the bar in HellBurger. I knew they only called me a degenerate bum because they loved me. Mitch, Pappy, Snotty in the kitchen. The noon lunch crowd had filed out, the mess was cleaned up, and Cynthia came to sit by me.

"You look like shit, Norbs."

"Oh, Cynthia, you have such a way with words. I knew you loved me more than Mitch."

She touched my arm, and I felt human for the first time since . . . well, you know when. "Yeah, I love you, man. You know I do." She hesitated and I was not sure I wanted her to say anything else because I knew what it was going to be. "You're not done yet, are you? I know you, Norby. You ain't gonna quit until it's all over. Be careful. These guys are mean and play with a different set of rules."

I leaned to her and kissed her forehead, got up and staggered to my Reliant. She was right. I wasn't going to quit.

Back in my office bedroom, I made an effort to test my physical abilities. As far as I got with push-ups was laying on the floor. "This is no good. I'm a slob and ain't gonna ever change." I managed to garner enough strength to stand up again, vowing never to go that low again. Physically, I was a wreck. Mentally, I was an idiot. That was what I had to work with.

In Grossy's office, I argued for twenty minutes to get my Ruger back. "It's evidence, you horse's butt. Get out of here."

"Stu, you're my closest friend. I earn my living as a private detective, and I need a gun. I passed all the tests, have a license to carry, and I frequent the shooting range to hone my professional skills. Besides, I know the case is closed."

I nagged him enough to make him cave in. After filling out too many unnecessary forms, I had the Ruger back. With an exception. "No, you can't have the silencer. That's for the crooks."

Understanding his skewed logic, I sarcastically said, "Well, we certainly don't want to inhibit the crooks by having citizens able to defend themselves. Next thing, we're gonna get sued by a mugger if we fight back." I was out of his office before the paper weight got to me.

I had some loose ends to tie up, and I kept remembering the weapon that killed Laura. The one I saw on the floor when the asshole tried to kill me. I knew where to find it and who had it.

Too much time had lapsed since Laura was killed, but I was in no hurry. My next step had to be better planned than blindly walking into a trap that tore my neck apart. Armed goons had been sent to my apartment, but I was not the target. They wanted Laura and the location of the bonds. I hadn't been bothered since I got out of the hospital, so I could naturally assume they had what they wanted, or they were planning a grand finale.

That would make good logic if it weren't for the guy tailing me.

I wasn't sure at first, but now I was positive. There are a lot of ways to drop a tail, but I needed to keep a connection to the head of this monster. If they were waiting to see if I was on my way to the bonds, all they were going to get was frustration. Laura never told me in so many words, but I had a pretty good idea where they were. And they weren't going anywhere.

I lost a boatload of extra weight in the hospital, trimming down from "fat ass" to "not bad." The biggest advantage was being able to move around without getting out of breath. I'd wear a scar around my neck forever, but since I didn't have any tattoos, I'd be right in style.

I wasn't sure what my next move was going to be in regards to my safety, or even my life, but at this point I didn't give a shit. I was keeping my living quarters in the office, and as long as I kept the door shut, Jeanine didn't mind. My office was as secure as it needed to be, and my files were locked up and couldn't be accessed by anything less than a direct hit by a very large bomb. Two days ago, I ran the film from the security cameras hidden through the office. What kind of a bone head breaks into the office of a private detective not thinking the place was bugged? It reeked of blind arrogance, and that was frightening.

I had finally decided I'd screwed around long enough and needed to get back to Adelle Pierpont. I was physically ready but in an emotional meltdown. I left my gun locked in the office, possibly one more stupid thing I did. But, when you got good at something, what the hey, do it often.

Chapter Nineteen

Why people live in these oversized mausoleums, I'd never understand. So far I was aware of two people living in the Pierpont place. Usually, after the impression of wealth and stature had been digested, those huge relics had leaky roofs, crumbling foundations, faulty electric, and defunct furnaces. Grand at the turn of an old century, but, for most, the wealth was all window dressing now.

The gate opened at my command, and I took up space under the portico. Pushing the button beside the door, I had no idea if it even worked. I came without an invitation, so if they were all in the money vault, counting, I'd be outside a long time. A dark-blue Pontiac sat at the curb keeping me under surveillance. I was tempted to go out and ask them in with me. I was sure they'd be welcome, as this was where their paycheck came from.

I stood in place for about half an hour, hitting the button every few minutes. On the verge of going into the bushes to pee, I was startled by signs of life on the other side of the door. Again, the incredibly gorgeous Kathleen stood in the opening, staring at me. Today she was clothed in extremely short shorts and a white tee shirt designed to be a tad too small and assigned to light up her nipples. Low-cut sneakers and no socks kept her feet off the bare floor. Those long curvy legs again, flowing from the sneakers to the crotch of the skimpy shorts.

Giving me a few very long moments to feel uncomfortable, and ogle her, she breathed out the words, "Mr. Klein, we weren't expecting you." She waited for an answer, but I didn't have one. I was beginning to think the seasons would change before I was invited in. Finally, she stepped aside. "Come in."

I was surprised and interested when, after closing the door, she slid the bolt to lock the door. Yes, statues talked, and this one did. "What was it you wanted?"

Behind my charming smile, I said, "I'd like to see your mother, please."

"You should have called first. She's indisposed at the moment."

Rocking on the balls of my feet, I answered, "Well, maybe you could un-indispose her. I think she's going to want to talk to me."

"Why would she want to talk to you? She doesn't need your services anymore."

I was being grilled, and this fountain of sensuous flesh was winding me up. She was manipulative and very good. Get me to take the lead, and she could control the conversation. I needed to eke an offering like tossing chum into the water to start a feeding frenzy. As much as I loved standing there raking her long naked legs with my eyes, I had to get to the next level.

"My dear Kathleen, we can stand here and volley all day if you want, but please go tell Adelle that I have the bonds."

Her face was frozen in that seductive pout she wore so well, matter-of-factly absorbing what I was feeding her. She stepped to me, but instead of wrapping her arms around me and sticking her tongue in my mouth, she said, "This way."

I was led into the same study this affair had begun in. "Please have a seat. This may take a moment." Her voice, still dripping with sex appeal, was firm and way too business like. Obediently, I sat.

The wait at the doorbell was nothing compared to the wait in the study. At least I was inside. I wandered into the hallway and spied a conspicuous door. I was right. A powder room, and the best of all, it had a toilet. The relief of expelling waste can be almost as good as some sex, knowing that it wasn't going down your leg. I dried my hands with a femmy-wemmy little towel, intentionally leaving it crumpled on the vanity. These people needed to learn how to live with a little flexibility.

Back in the study, I browsed, but there was nothing incriminating, let alone interesting. This room and Kathleen's bedroom were the only places I've been welcomed into. After sex-pot's bedroom, I didn't care if there were any more rooms.

I chose a wing back chair upholstered in a rich satin to plant myself in. I became drowsy. My last thought was not to drool on the chair.

Kathleen's crisp voice woke me up. "Mr. Klein, my mother will be here in a moment. Sit up and look presentable." The chastising put me back in Ms Westby's English class. If Kathleen pulled out a ruler to belt me with, I'd be home in a sea of high school memories. Shaking the sleep away, I noted Kathleen sitting behind the large leather-covered desk. I was wondering if Adelle still grounded her daughter for indiscretions.

After a sociable amount of time being glared at by sex-pot, the grand matriarch made her entrance. I expected a fanfare by uniformed serfs, but what staggered into the room was less than elegant. She looked as old as she was, disheveled gray hair, no make up, and dressed in a dowdy old dress, faded years ago. A perfect match for Hanky. If it weren't for the cane, she would have fallen over. The cane. Yes, the cane. I was worried it wouldn't show up.

Since the desk was occupied, Adelle sat in a straight-backed Windsor chair, clutching the cane between her knees. Looking deep into her eyes, I saw it. Mrs. Adelle Pierpont was either stoned or drunk. Her gravely voice lacked the authority to make me submissive, "Mr. Klein, Kathleen says you have the bonds." Reaching her bird claw hand out, she snapped her fingers. "Now, you miserable wretch. Give them to me."

My fingers steepled in front of my mouth kept my confusion and utter disappointment hidden. The old lady was smashed. Leaning forward, I started my dissertation on the downfall of noble enterprises. "Mrs. Pierpont, you don't look well. Is there anything you need? Water? Aspirin? Black coffee?"

Kathleen sat forward, looking concerned. She should be.

Adelle sat forward as well, only a little. I thought she would teapot out of the chair. Her voice became but a hiss. "How dare you come in here and talk like that."

"Adelle. May I call you Adelle? After what we've gone through together, I should be allowed a little freedom of familiarity."

Louder, her voice cracking, she said, "You ignorant swine . . ."

"Swine, maybe. Ignorant, I don't think so. You hired me to find the bonds, and I've done that. Only half, but since you have the cash from the other half, I feel I've done a good job."

Kathleen was taking a deep interest in this exchange. I leveled again at Adelle. "I've been tortured, shot, and choked, all in an attempt to get the bonds. I was left for dead twice. You need to hire better goons to do your dirty work."

Kathleen broke in, "The bonds, Mr. Klein, where are they?"

"Are they really that important? Elwood lost them, and some Arab is putting together a hit squad because he was supposed to buy weapons to kill Americans. And you're frantic to get them so you aren't subjected to whatever Arabs do to cheats and thieves. I guess though, that you made a deal with the Arabs by handing over the cash and covered the rest of the bonds from your own assets. Otherwise, that dope you have tailing me would have acted sooner."

That little bit of news got them both upset. Weakly, Adelle tried to cover her mistake. "I don't know what you're talking about."

"Yes, you do. Laura didn't give them up even after she was tortured. You had to slit her throat to put an end to it. When I shot Elmer Fudd in the hallway of my apartment building, whoever you hired got cold feet. Now, the only connection you have to the bonds is me. And you think you need to be easy since I've proven to be a more formidable opponent than you anticipated. I was supposed to be waxed as soon as I handed over the bonds, but your husband's lust got in the way."

Adelle was shaking, her hands clenched to the cane. "You can't prove anything."

"I really don't have to, but I can."

Kathleen stood up, and I never realized how tall she was, and I saw the strength in her bearing. She moved around the desk, coming to stand too close to me. In a firm and authoritative voice, she asked again, "Give us the bonds, Norbert. We can make a very handsome deal with you."

There it was again. I hated the proper use of my name. "Please, call me Norby."

Louder, Kathleen yelped, "I'll call you dead if you don't turn them over. I mean it."

I stood facing her, a few feet away, which was exactly where she wanted me. Maybe they were right, I was an ignorant swine. I started to make my deal, "My dear Kathleen, you already tried to kill me twice and got nowhere."

All I saw was the sole of her sneaker shooting through space, then collapsing as it landed on my chest. "Oh, shit." I had no air left in my lungs. I gasped and inhaled like the intake on a blast furnace. I could imagine catching a sixteen-pound bowling ball shot out of a cannon. I was surprised that I was able to stand, becoming upright with plans to return the blow. While I was busy being dumb, I looked up and saw Kathleen leap out to drive the heel of her hand into my face. I flew, yes, *flew*, off my feet to slam against the door. Splayed across the large oak panel, I saw more coming at me. She spun in a perfect Jackie Chan move, and her sneaker, at the end of that perfectly sculptured leg that at one time squeezed my face between it and the other one, strike home by crushing my skull. I spun to the left, arms flailing like a clown's, smashing into something very hard and sharp. I slid down the side of the armoire I had crashed into, crumpling on the floor.

Wiping the flood of blood from my eyes, I saw my certain death as the next step. Kathleen, yanked the cane away from Adelle. Her mother yelled, "No, don't. Not here."

Kathleen stood with a wide stance holding the cane in both hands. If she hit me with it, I'd thank her. But, there was a different plan. The cane was not a cane, but a Laguiole knife. She grasped the silver knurled handle like it was the organ on King Kong, and pulled it from the scabbard posing as a cane. The blade was at least ten inches long, looked sharp, and gleamed through the sweat and blood covering my face. The same silver knurled knife I had seen on the floor when I found Laura. The same knife that killed the ambassador's chauffer. The silver knurled handle on the cane that the Pierpont matriarch held so closely was now in the hands of vengeful beauty, hell-bent on killing me.

Struggling to get my legs under me instead of spread out like a daddy-long-leg spider, it was taking too long and at too much effort. Through the fog, I heard a scream. A high-pitched wail that sounded like it was coming through sandpaper. "Kathleen, stop. This is madness. Please don't."

The love of my life, the beautiful Kathleen, turned to her mother, and swung the cane into her head. Screaming, her arms taut with those marvelous muscles flexing, Kathleen let it fly, "Shut up, you stupid hag. Shut your fucking mouth. I earned every cent of that money while you sat here crapping in your pants looking like some goddamn queen. Every one thinks you're so high and mighty. The Pierpont bitch that they think is in control." Bringing the cane back over her shoulder, Kathleen tensed for a last blow to the emaciated old woman lying on the floor.

Somehow I managed to croak loud enough to get Kathleen's attention. "Stop. It doesn't have to go any further." Sitting with my back against the armoire, I held my hand out expecting a dove and crown of laurel leaves in a grand gesture of peace. I steadied the spinning room and pleaded, "You can have it all. Don't kill her." My voice lacked the authority I had hoped for, but with my blood pouring through a hole in my face, and probably all my ribs shattered, it was all I could do to work my way up the armoire to stand up. Staying alive wasn't even an issue now. I didn't know what the issue was, but I did know this woman had to stop what she was doing.

Kathleen, turning to me, had the look of pure hate and evil, red eyes and all. She dropped the cane and fondled the knife. I really wish she'd stop that. "You. You slimy piece of shit. You were supposed to be dead a long time ago. You were a patsy, you dumb fuck. If it wasn't for that whore, I'd be worth a fortune now."

Desperate to make some logic she could handle, I whined, "You still can. You will have everything. If you kill me you'll never find the bonds. I don't want them. They're too much trouble, and I wouldn't know what to do with them."

She slashed the air in front of me, trying to scare me, and it had amazing results. All I could do was flinch. Screaming, she made her point. "You cashed them, dumb ass. Or did you forget that?"

"Laura cashed them, not me. I tried to get them from her, but she was too stubborn. Her plan was to cash a couple and give the rest back. When we were trying to figure out who was chasing us, she got scared and told me where she put them. Put the knife down, and we can get them. They belong to you, not me."

Without warning, her foot came flying at me so fast it may have broken the speed of light law. All I felt was the floor hitting me, and my head collapsing. The slime and blood were flowing faster than coagulation could do its job.

Her next act was the final one. On my back I felt her knee crush my broken ribs and the pain sent me on a surreal trip to more pain. My last thoughts on earth should have been seeing Cheryl all over again, angelic and clean. Instead I processed the picture of Kathleen with her knee dug into the back of her father, pulling on the leather strap. I saw the driver in the Cadillac get the knife drawn over his throat. And most vividly, I saw Kathleen instructing her henchmen to tie up Laura, then torture her and try to sever her head. The leather cutting into my neck was next.

My one good eye opened to see the maniacal woman straddling me as only Kathleen could, her knee killing me, and holding the silver handled knife against my throat. I thought she'd be disappointed because all my blood was pouring out my face.

Clutching my hair to force my head back, she knew I was helpless to stop her. I had nothing to offer myself to stop this. Then I heard the shot and saw Kathleen lurch, a stunned expression on her face. My blood was all over her now, coating her legs, soaking the shorts and tee shirt. There was another shot, this one close, but it slammed into the door frame. Then one more, and Kathleen groaned, looked at me and spit on me. She fell forward on top of me, the knife still clenched in her hand. With her knee off me I managed to turn to the side, toppling her over.

If it weren't for the pain poking me, I would have slipped into a coma, or death. Crawling away from my death spot on the floor, I looked up and saw Adelle, flat on her ass on the floor, the gun still in her hand. I crawled to her, not to comfort her, but to get the gun away.

When I had shuffled myself to her, she tucked the gun behind her back. Oh, swell. Wincing, oh, man, that hurt, I croaked, "Adelle, give me the gun."

She blinked and looked at me. Her face was swollen and bleeding from a gash across her cheek. There was a collection of broken teeth in her lap. The old dowdy dress. She opened her mouth but it took a few more tries before she spoke.

Chapter Twenty

●●●●●●●●●●●●●●●●●●●●

"ADELLE, THE GUN. GIVE IT TO ME."

I wasn't even on the same planet with her. The babbling started and she couldn't stop. "She was in control of the house. The syndicate was hers. She gave the orders." Adelle hesitated, breathless, but she continued on. "She had always been a problem. Her father abused her since she was seven. At eleven she got pregnant and had an abortion in Sweden. As she got older and more beautiful, she took charge of everything. She used me as a front. Most of the time I was kept drugged and locked up. What you saw here was an act she forced me into. The night she killed Elwood, she came home and danced in front me, naked. She was sick."

Panting, she again opened her mouth to speak, but I interrupted, "Adelle, don't go into it. You can be saved."

She looked at me and laughed. "You're stupid. By having to make up for the bonds we had to cover, we're penniless. You don't have them or you and that whore would be gone."

"I do have them, Adelle. I don't want them. Give me the gun, and we can end this."

She wasn't done. She needed to get rid of what was grinding inside her head. This was a confession and I was her confessor. "My husband was bent on power. When he was brought home from his term as ambassador, he set up the syndicate. Contacts he made in the Arab world used him as a way to get American weapons. He was having an affair with Kathleen, his own daughter. He became enamored of her and allowed her to take control of what he set up. She became too powerful and discovered he was trying to get rid of her. That was when she killed him."

More disenchanted than exhausted, the old woman, still sitting still on the floor, rolled her head and moaned, "It was all so horrible."

Myself, I wasn't all too certain I was going to live long enough to get some help over here. Adelle was busy moaning and lamenting on what a horseshit life she'd had, and that was fine. What bothered me was the gun, which she had started waving around like a pointer at a lecture. Pulling myself across the carpet to the desk, my target was the telephone. Totally unable to stand up, I pulled on the cord hanging over the side of the desk. The phone came off the desk to land on my head. "Oh, shit."

Adelle was oblivious of life around her, her only connection to earth was the revolver she held like a new toy. The telephone cracking my skull made me even more totally useless. Lying on the carpet, I pulled the phone to me, fumbled with the buttons, and hoped beyond life itself that I had found 911. The receiver was on the floor next to me. I heard a tiny voice ask me what I wanted. As loud as I could, I eked out a really wimpy, "Help." That wasn't good enough, so I tried yelling, and that really hurt. "The Pierpont house, on London Road. People dead. Hurry." What I was offering wasn't good enough to arouse a 911 interest, but the gun shot worked just fine.

Startled by the explosion, I looked at Adelle, who was now lying in her own pool of blood. Seeing what a bullet does to a person's head as it comes out the other side was not a pleasant sight. Her face still looked like the frozen matriarch she had been posed to be, but the left half of her head was hamburger. I looked back to the door where I had gotten my ass kicked to taunt the dead Kathleen with a "Nya Nya," but all that was there was blood-soaked carpeting. She was gone. Again, all I could muster was, "Oh, shit".

I heard the sirens. The cavalry had arrived. The clods were out there ringing the doorbell, waiting for someone to let them in. I wasn't the dumbest Crayola in the box anymore. "Break it down. Set fire to it. Get in here." I expected a loud crash from the heavy door being assaulted, but there were just feet running, running through the house calling, "Klein? Mrs. Pierpont? Anyone?"

Finally, bursting into the study, the golden warbling of my friend, Detective Stu Grosslein, came closer. "Klein, what's going on here? Did you make the call?" Looking back at the blood and the remnants of Adelle, all he could think of to say was, "Jesus."

An EMT wrapped my head with two miles of gauze and tried to get me onto a stretcher. Grossy was still trying to be a cop, asking, "Klein, what the hell did you do here?"

I wanted to die, or at least pass out, to get me out of a painful, cloudy situation, and this dope wanted a conversation. I reached up and grabbed his tie, pulling him down to my level. "Grossy, don't be an asshole. Kathleen Pierpont killed the ambassador, the guy in the car, and Laura. She tried to kill me, but her mother shot her."

The EMT, obviously better at his job than Grossy, got a little too anxious. He told Stu, "We gotta get him in the rig. Talk to him at the hospital."

Using Grossy's tie, I pulled myself upright and staggered. "No, no ambulance. We have to find Kathleen Pierpont." I tried, as loud as I could, rattling my warning to Stu, "She's hurt and running. Stop her."

Weaving my way to the door, my foot hit the shaft of the cane. With great effort, I squatted to pick it up. The knife was gone. Clutching the wooden shaft, I made my way to the front door. Grossy was behind calling me names. The front door stood wide open, covered with blood and Kathleen's hand print. I turned to an excited Grossy, asking, "The door. When you got here, was the door open?"

"Yeah. Just like it is."

I stepped outside and looked through the iron fence into the street. The dark-blue Pontiac was gone. Logic would have it taking off when the circus of flashing lights and police cars stormed the palace, but my thinking had it taking the wounded Kathleen away.

Grabbing Grossy by the lapel of his cheap suit, I yelled, "A dark-blue Pontiac. It took her away. You gotta find it."

Assuring me he would put out an APB on Kathleen and the Pontiac, my legs turned into pudding, and I hit the turf, my lights out for a long time.

I was getting used to the hospital routine, and since Attila the Hun wasn't one of my nurses, I enjoyed the evening rubs and toilet training. I spent a very long time giving the same report to about twelve different teams of police, each making its own report.

Of particular importance to me was having Jeanine show up to tell me she had taken over the business and hired a partner she could work with. She said that since I was famous now, they were keeping my name on the letterhead as a stimulus. She showed me her new business card that really had my name on it, although now I had been reduced to "associate." I asked if she would reconsider putting the title of "pimp" back on it, but she was too busy laughing to answer me.

"Jeanine, I have favor."

Her answer, "Anything but oral sex."

"Oh, well, then I have another favor. Would you get my Reliant and put it a storage garage? Put a lock on the door. I don't want anyone stealing the new tires."

This time it took almost a whole month to be able to join society again. Jeanine, with the interference of Mrs. Feldstein, redecorated my apartment. A new bed, painted walls, carpeting and a vacuum cleaner, and even a coffee pot that had controls on it that came from the cockpit of a 747 and no mouse turds inside. I asked her, "What does this do?"

"It makes coffee, bonehead."

"That's like cooking, isn't it?"

"Only if you aren't too stupid to pour water into it and press the brew button."

My next question was of a personal nature. "Uh, Jeanine, who's the . . . guy hanging around?"

At the mention of him being in the room, he pranced to me and brightly announced, "Hi there. I'm Claude, your nurse. I'll be helping you get to a speedy recovery in no time at all." He extended his arm with a limp hand attached to it. All I could bring myself to do was to touch it.

Claude and Mrs. Feinstein did wonders to make me healthy with chicken soup and constantly annoying me. Together they exchanged recipes and gossip from Oprah and Lindsey Lohan. Claude taught my ample neighbor how to embroider and a neat trick to use in cross stitch. What's that?

My visits with Grossy were more congenial, and he surprised the crap out of me when he asked, "Think you might want to be a paid consultant for the department? The commissioner is impressed that you broke up a gang they didn't know anything about."

"Gee, Grossy, someone does love me. I'll think about it." Of greater importance, I asked, "What about Kathleen Pierpont? If she's alive, she'll be coming back here. She's one pissed-off babe who still has the murder weapon."

Detective Grosslein had been forced into this position and he didn't like it. I was being offered a job as a police consultant to put me in the spotlight. Bait for the missing and vengeful, although beautiful, Kathleen. "We're looking, Norbs. She's vanished, which means she had some cash stashed to finance her disappearance. Your talking about that dark-blue Pontiac also means she's not alone."

Satisfied that I had done my civic duty, I made my way out to my former office, where I had now become an associate. The place had changed. My eclectically designed office was now a walnut-paneled conference room with carpeting. The outer office had two matching desks with matching ornaments neatly arranged on top. There was a small table in the back corner with a box of garbage on it. My new nameplate was on it also. "Don't I even get a desk?"

The new partner, named Bruin Heinz, greeted me, "What do you want? You don't need a desk." I expected her to grab her crotch and spit. Her voice was deep and booming, and I was sure she could lead an army through Europe.

Jeanine stepped in to keep her from kicking my ass. I couldn't survive another attack. "Norbs, this is Bruin, my associate, and your working partner. Call her Brew and you'll get along just fine."

Brew stood about six-foot-three and had a body constructed of sculpted muscle and more muscle. She sported an artificial tan, and every time she moved, something on her flexed. I found her strangely attractive, in a deadly way. I was sure she ate hot rivets and drank malt liquor for breakfast. When she and Jeanine did a wet-lip kiss, I knew I really was out of the picture.

Lying, I told her, "Glad to meet you." I didn't offer to shake her hand because it was bigger than mine. Smiling a peace offering, I added, "I just came in to get the key to the storage garage. I'm going to pick up my car now."

Brew drove me to the storage garage. Before I was able to escape, she clamped on to my arm, "You going to come back into the office?"

The pain shooting up my arm made me grimace. I answered, "I don't know for sure, but I won't get in the way. I promise."

Happy to see Grunhilda drive away, I opened the overhead door to the garage. There it was, sitting in all the regal glory. A classic. The new tires still had a pleasant smell, like a good deodorant. Caressing the oxidized paint, I went to the driver's door and squatted in front of the opening. The dome light came on so I was reasonably sure it had enough battery to start.

Running my hand under the driver's side of the front seat I felt the bracket where I had kept my back-up .32. Of course the bracket was empty, but there was something else there. I fondled it and smiled. My Laura, ever so resourceful. I took it out and gazed at a storage locker key from the bus depot. Number 202. Yes, God loves me and allowed the Reliant to cough itself into life.

I circled the city a few times and didn't spot a tail. Hoping my powers of observation were astute, I pulled into the bus depot. Still watching for a spook, I found locker number 202 and cranked the door open.

The only thing inside was Laura's large purse. Filled with green scrolled documents. Of more importance to me was the hand written note. *Dear Norby, If you get to this note, it will obviously mean I'm dead. I'm sure you will untangle the puzzle and I'm sorry I can't be with you to enjoy this. I wasn't meant to be alive very long anyway, and I'm okay with that. I can pass on peaceably knowing that asshole Billy went first. Thank you for sticking with me and trying to help. I can never tell you how much that meant. If I had known you years ago, I'd have had a totally different life. My Love, Laura.*

Chapter Twenty-One

I GAVE THE PURSE TO CLAUDE, AND HE JOYFULLY SANG about going out to find a matching outfit. Here I was sitting on a fortune, and I didn't want it. However, I was not nearly as stupid as I looked. I salted away a couple of the bonds for myself and tried to do some good with the rest. Mrs. Feldstein got a mysterious envelope with a deposit slip from a bank nearby. Hanky refused any money. I gave the local liquor store a bundle, asking that Hanky be kept in enough Silver Satin and Mad Dog to swim in. Doing a little checking, I came across a battered women's shelter that tried to transform prostitutes. The lack of funding hadn't allowed them much success. Now, they can hire a counselor and offer a scholarship to get an education. They agreed to call it the Laura Blake fund.

Jeanine and her muscular partner were now able to finance a full detective agency, and out of appreciation they agreed to keep my name on the letterhead. The rest went to an orphanage in Duluth, expanding the Laura Blake scholarship.

On my back burner of unfinished business, I knew I had to go to San Diego. The least I could do was to visit Marci's grave site and say hello to her daughter, Jennifer. It was a short, sad trip, and I came home the same day I got there.

I found a used Winnebago and had a hitch and brake control added. A dandy fourteen-foot runabout with a ten-horse Evinrude finished it off just fine. Loaded with beer, booze, and frozen pizza, my friend Stu Grosslein and I took off for an extended vacation in the little town of Hovland, north of Grand Marais, Minnesota. An obscure little town on the shore of Lake Superior, it was the perfect hideaway.

Those twenty-pound lake trout were elusive, but with patience and a desire not to work it too hard, they can be had. The Chicago Bay restaurant, in

Hovland, agreed to cook up some trout for us with the rest as a dinner special for their evening dinner crowd.

Too soon, Stu had to get back to work, and we headed back, tired, but singing all the way. Dropping him off at home, he wouldn't get out until I gave him an answer.

"C'mon, Norbs, the commissioner is pressing me to get you on board as a consultant. You'll get paid and get all the bennies that go with it. You can even carry a gun."

I rested my head on the steering wheel and sighed, "All right. But, I want my own business card with the title of 'pimp' on it."

Back in the crime-solving business I set up my office at the end of the bar in HellBurger. There was a space on the wall for those little yellow sticky notes, and since I had a bank account now, I was able to start a tab. I had my own business cards printed, but when I got them back I was horrified to see the title of pimp had been left off. So with a pencil, I wrote it in on all five-hundred of them.

I was conspicuous on purpose. Exposing myself, I hoped to draw out Laura's killer, and regardless of the lottery going on as to when I'd get my throat slashed, I was keeping my eyes open. At some point, Kathleen was going to get too angry to hide anymore and show up. I was going to be ready when she did. Until then, my annex office in HellBurger was open. I was surrounded by good booze, good friends, and good . . . exposure.

If you're ever in Canal Park, stop in and see me. No appointment needed.

Authors Note

Cynthia Gerdes and Mitch Omer

Yes, Hell Burger was a real place, and Cynthia and Mitch are real people. The economic downward spiral closed the doors to Hell Burger in October 2010. The staff that made the place an iconic presence in the area was a close-knit group, and several have moved with Mitch and Cyn to their ongoing adventure, Hells Kitchen, located in downtown Minneapolis. From his table-dancing escapades to the motorcycle episode, and his adventurous life in between, Mitch is a story by himself.

Cyn is an outgoing and warm loving lady, but to best describe Mitch—If Neil Cassady, and Jack Kerouac, were to take another bus ride to California, Mitch would be on that bus.

My wife and I enjoying the ambience at Hells Kitchen
www.hellskitcheninc.com

The front of the original Hell Burger
in Duluth, Minnesota.